SPECIAL MESSAGE TO READERS

This book is published under the auspices of

THE ULVERSCROFT FOUNDATION

(registered charity No. 264873 UK)

Established in 1972 to provide funds for research, diagnosis and treatment of eye diseases. Examples of contributions made are: —

A Children's Assessment Unit at Moorfield's Hospital, London.

•

Twin operating theatres at the Western Ophthalmic Hospital, London.

•

A Chair of Ophthalmology at the Royal Australian College of Ophthalmologists.

•

The Ulverscroft Children's Eye Unit at the Great Ormond Street Hospital For Sick Children, London.

You can help further the work of the Foundation by making a donation or leaving a legacy. Every contribution, no matter how small, is received with gratitude. Please write for details to:

THE ULVERSCROFT FOUNDATION,
The Green, Bradgate Road, Anstey,
Leicester LE7 7FU, England.
Telephone: (0116) 236 4325

In Australia write to:
THE ULVERSCROFT FOUNDATION,
c/o The Royal Australian College of
Ophthalmologists,
27, Commonwealth Street, Sydney,
N.S.W. 2010.

SEA TANGLE

When Jenny Duff accepted the offer of a temporary job in a small Ayrshire seaside village, she fell in love with Lethansea — and with one of the inhabitants, Robin Maxwell. Yet, somehow, Jenny could never get away from the shadow of Beryl McLean, a girl whom she had never met but who seemed to be a constant barrier between herself and Robin. What was the mystery surrounding Beryl? Would it in the end ruin Jenny's happiness?

MARY CUMMINS

♦

SEA TANGLE

Complete and Unabridged

LINFORD
Leicester

First published in Great Britain

First Linford Edition
published 2000

All the characters in this book have no existence
outside the imagination of the Author, and have
no relation whatsoever to anyone bearing the
same name or names. They are not even
distantly inspired by any individual known or
unknown to the Author, and all the incidents
are pure invention.

British Library CIP Data

Cummins, Mary
    Sea tangle.—Large print ed.—
    Linford romance library
    1. Love stories
    2. Large type books
    I. Title
    823.9'14 [F]

    ISBN 0–7089–5660–2

Published by
F. A. Thorpe (Publishing) Ltd.
Anstey, Leicestershire

Set by Words & Graphics Ltd.
Anstey, Leicestershire
Printed and bound in Great Britain by
T. J. International Ltd., Padstow, Cornwall

This book is printed on acid-free paper

1

It was her first proposal of marriage.

Jenny Duff looked away from the man sitting beside her on the settee, and caught sight of herself in the large old-fashioned sideboard mirror. She was twenty-five, but looked older, with tired lines on her pale face, and brownish hair which was dull and lifeless. If she wanted her own home, and children, this was probably her last chance . . . and she'd dreamed of this moment many times . . .

'You can't go to this place . . . what did you call it?'

'Lethansea.'

'Lethansea. A tiny village, from what you say, Jenny, when your home has always been in Glasgow. Now that it's all over, why can't you stay on here, in this house? It's bigger than my flat, and I'd have no objection to taking it over from you, darling, and living here. It's a bit old now, but spacious and roomy, and I like that. It seems ill-considered to me, to let this house, and go off to the wilds somewhere where you'll have to live in digs.'

'Lethansea isn't in the wilds, Charles. It's only sixty miles from here, and on the coast, too. It's a lovely little village.'

Jenny looked into Charles Cairns' sulky face. If only he'd asked her a year ago, or even six months, she'd have been happy to say yes. They'd been colleagues at a large nearby grammar school, where Jenny taught English and Charles was games master to the boys.

Jenny had given up her job to nurse her mother when she became ill after a heart attack. Charles' support in the dark days of uncertainty, and the long tiring hours of nursing besides trying to run the home, would have been a haven for her. But although he had kept in touch and had called to see her, bringing an occasional bunch of flowers for the sickroom, he had never discussed a future together. He had waited till Mrs. Duff died, and Jenny was left alone.

She hadn't, however, been left penniless. Jenny had been rather relieved to find her financial situation much better than she'd feared, and old Mr. Prentice, the lawyer, had been quick to point out that the house, which was large and well furnished, would also bring in a good sum of money if Jenny decided to sell.

'I don't know, Mr. Prentice,' she had told him, tiredly. 'I . . . I'll have to think about it.'

'Perhaps a good holiday . . . '

She had shaken her head. She knew very few people who would be willing or able to have her to stay, and she didn't welcome the prospect of going to a hotel on her own.

'You could do with a visit to your doctor,' Mr. Prentice told her, looking with sympathy at the pale young woman. She was only the same age as his own daughter who, in spite of a husband and two young children, looked years younger than Jenny Duff.

'Dr. John . . . Dr. John Murdoch, you know . . . he's been very good. Maybe I will see him,' promised Jenny. 'Thank you, Mr. Prentice.'

'Let me know your plans, my dear,' the old man told her kindly.

Jenny had gone to see Dr. John, who greeted her kindly when she walked into his surgery.

'Sit down, my dear,' he said quickly. 'As a matter of fact, I'd had it in mind to call and see you, only I've been so busy . . . '

'I know,' Jenny nodded. 'I've seen the surgery.'

Dr. John nodded ruefully, and ran a hand through his thick grey hair.

'I've been thinking about you, nevertheless. Your mother's illness put a strain on you, and you could do with getting away for a real change. Have you any plans, Jenny?'

4

She shook her head.

'I don't really want a holiday on my own, and there's nobody I want to go to. I . . . I thought of asking for my old job back at the Grammar School. I know they're short of teachers, but the Principal probably won't want me until September.'

Dr. John tapped thoughtfully on his blotter with the back of his pen, then wrote out a prescription.

'Here's a tonic for you, anyway. Does it have to be Glasgow, Jenny? . . . the teaching, I mean? I have a suggestion to put to you, and I want you to think about it for a few days. My brother's a doctor, too, you know, only he's got a country practice at Lethansea. You might not know the place, but it's south of Ayr, near the coast, and a fine place for putting some good sea air into your lungs. Apparently the school is only a small place with two teachers. The headmaster and his wife live at the school house, and he teaches the older children. He and my brother, Neil, are cronies. I've met him a few times myself. Adam Paterson is a good man and has sent some fine pupils into the schools in Ayr after he's trained them up to standard. He has a young teacher taking the young ones, a Miss McLean . . . Beryl McLean. Unfortunately, or maybe fortunately for her, Beryl's sister who lives in Canada has asked the girl to come and stay. She's got leave of absence for two terms.'

Dr. John paused and looked to see how Jenny was taking all this information, but although she met his gaze with interest, she made no comment, and he sighed and reached for a letter on his desk.

'How about it, Jenny?' he asked bluntly. 'Two terms teaching the wee ones at Lethansea. It will give you a change of scene, good sea air, something to do, and it will help out Adam Paterson at the same time. Here's all the information from my brother. It gives you the address where you've to write if you want to take it on. I suppose you *can* teach the little ones as well as older children? There are so many rules and regulations these days, I get fair lost amongst them all.'

Jenny was nodding.

'I taught in Primary School before deciding to specialise in English . . . '

She broke off, her eyes still troubled. This idea of Dr. John's was new to her, but nonetheless attractive. She recognised now that she really wanted to get away from Glasgow for a little while, but the thought of having nothing to do had been abhorrent to her. This new idea offered her a challenge, and a complete break, and she rose slowly to her feet.

'I *will* think about it, Dr. John,' she promised, 'but I feel I can't thank you enough for your help. This offer sounds very attractive and if I could . . . could get a temporary job like this, I . . . I'm sure I'd love to tackle it.'

The old man beamed with pleasure. He was very fond of Jenny Duff, and sad to see that the sparkle had gone out of the girl over the past few months. Jenny might never have been exactly beautiful, but he'd often thought that her broad sweet brow with the pale brown hair and amber eyes had given her an elusive quality which had made her seem attractive and, in fact, rather lovely. Now it was as though a lamp had been dimmed, and that Jenny walked in the shadow of her former self.

'Come and see me next week,' Dr. John invited. 'Tell me what you've done about it.'

'All right, Dr. John.'

★ ★ ★

Jenny had given herself two days to consider, then she applied for the temporary job and had been found suitable for the position. She had paid a flying visit to Lethansea one Saturday, and had briefly met Mr. Paterson who showed her over the

8

school, which seemed very tiny after the large grammar school in Glasgow.

But Jenny had liked the place on sight, and had gone back to Glasgow to arrange the letting of her house. Mr. Paterson had taken her along to meet Mrs. Beattie Sinclair, who was willing to let her a room in her pretty cottage, and Jenny had been more than willing to accept.

Her new plans had gone with a swing, and she had only thought about Charles Cairns with the back of her mind, realising that she would have to let him know she was leaving.

Charles had been calling on Jenny more frequently since her mother died, and had been rather worried about her until after she had seen Mr. Prentice.

'There's really no need to worry, Charles,' she told him that evening. 'I shall have an income, even if it's small, and Mr. Prentice thinks the house would bring in a good sum. The furniture is antique, too, and Daddy bought a few good pictures, so I shan't be hard up.'

Charles drew a breath of satisfaction and leaned back in his chair to fumble for a cigarette.

'I'm so glad, Jenny,' he told her, 'and I shouldn't be in any hurry to sell the house if I were you.' He looked round the large spacious drawing-room appreciatively. 'I've always liked your house, Jenny. It would be a pity to let it go.'

Jenny nodded, saying nothing. It would be a wrench to part with her home, but she felt its emptiness now that she was on her own. It was easy to remember the happy days of her childhood, and to be sad that they had gone for ever. Sometimes she was filled with an overwhelming desire to get away so that she could start again on a new life, and keep only the happy memories in her heart.

Dr. John's idea had been like a gift to her, and for a short while she had decided that she would sell the house, then caution had asserted itself, and

Jenny decided to let it instead.

That evening Charles had called, bringing a large box of chocolates, and Jenny welcomed him warmly, glad that she could now tell him her plans without having to write.

Only Charles hadn't been at all thrilled when she told him all about Lethansea. He looked at her with consternation.

'But you can't go just like that, Jenny. I . . . I came this evening to ask you to marry me.'

Jenny had been rather taken aback, and Charles began to grow impatient.

'I said I'd like to marry you, Jenny. I really mean it, too. We . . . we could arrange a wedding shortly, and if you want to go on with your career, why not apply for your old job back? You're sure to get it, you know.'

Jenny bit her lip. At one time it would have meant a great deal to her, but now there was something wrong with this proposal. Charles had said nothing about love, and she . . . she looked searchingly into his face . . . she didn't really love him either. And a treacherous thought kept popping into her mind that he hadn't proposed until after he knew she wouldn't exactly be destitute.

'I'm sorry, Charles,' she said, gently but firmly, 'but I must say no. We don't really love each other . . . '

'I do love you, Jenny,' Charles broke in, hurriedly. 'If that's all that's troubling you . . . '

'No, there's more. You see, I don't love you either, so it wouldn't work.'

Charles looked as though he didn't quite believe her.

'But people marry for other reasons than love, Jenny. I mean . . . we aren't youngsters, by any means, and sometimes a marriage built on good sound common sense and a healthy respect for one another is built on more solid ground than love's young dream.'

Jenny flushed. Was there a slightly sarcastic note in Charles' voice? No doubt he longed to remind her that she was no longer very young, and never had been very beautiful.

Her chin lifted and she looked at him squarely.

'I'm sorry, Charles,' she said quietly. 'I appreciate what you're offering, but I just can't accept.'

'You need time to consider,' Charles told her comfortingly, coming to put his arms round her. 'You've had too much to worry about recently. That's why I think it would be a mistake to rush off somewhere until you give yourself time to really know what you want. You may hate it at that new place . . . Lethansea . . .'

'I don't think so.'

He stood up for a moment, dropping his arms heavily to his sides.

'At least let me write to you. Give me your new address, then I can keep in touch, and perhaps come and see you now and again.'

'Yes, that would be nice,' she agreed, and went over to her desk to write it

13

down. 'I shall enjoy hearing from you, Charles, so long as you realise we can only be friends.'

After he had gone, Jenny sat down rather shakily and wondered if she had done the right thing. Had Charles been right in saying that a marriage based on common sense and respect would have suited both of them so much better? She had known Charles Cairns a long time and at one time she had even imagined herself in love with him.

Perhaps she was still in love with him, only her feeling had become dulled under the pain of her mother's illness, and the long hours of looking after her. When she felt better, would she be sorry she had sent Charles away?

The house felt unbearably lonely as she went up to bed, and she had to remind herself again how lucky she was to have it, and not to have the worry of earning her bread and butter immediately. Yet she was poor in a way which mattered most, in the comfort of a loving family and friends.

Jenny woke, heavy-eyed, next morning, but her mind was clearer and again it seemed that Lethansea was offering her a challenge. She was young and had her health, she reminded herself, as she splashed cold water on her face.

She would never have been sure how much Charles really wanted *her*, and nothing else. She had made the right decision, and now she looked forward to her new life.

2

Jenny made the last part of her journey to Lethansea by local bus from Ayr Bus Station.

She was rather tired because Charles had insisted on taking her out for a meal the night before. It hadn't been a success. Jenny had been slightly keyed up over the prospect of her journey next day, and hadn't been able to muster up too much interest over Charles, and she had been even less forthcoming when he again told her of his intention to keep in touch, and his belief that she would soon come round to the idea of marriage.

The restaurant was small and quiet and, Jenny suspected, not very expensive. The pretty young waitress was obviously inexperienced and Charles had glared at her, reprimanding her sharply for serving the food clumsily. Now all that Jenny could remember of the meal was the girl's wide brown eyes and her small childish face growing scarlet, then very pale.

'Please, Charles, it's all right,' Jenny had pleaded.

'There's too much inefficiency these days,' he said, rather pompously, and the girl walked away a trifle shakily. Jenny could only remember the incident with distaste.

But now she was having a delightful bus journey with fine views of the coast, and a warm welcome at the end of it from Mrs. Sinclair. She had written to say which train she would catch, and the older woman had accurately judged her bus time, and was waiting for her at the bus stop nearest her cottage.

'Just let me breathe the fresh sea air,' Jenny said, breathing deeply, as the bus rattled off, leaving them on their own. 'What a lovely afternoon.'

'Aye, it's a bonny day, though the wind blows cold from the sea. I've got a good meal ready for you, Miss Duff.'

Jenny's appetite had been poor of late, but she began to feel she could do justice to Mrs. Sinclair's meal as they walked along the quiet road near the sea front to the small cottage, vividly fresh with white and yellow paint, and frilled nylon curtains at the window.

'What's that?' asked Jenny, pointing towards the small natural harbour.

'What? Where?'

Mrs. Sinclair peered, a trifle short-sightedly.

'Och, that's the fishing nets hung out. You can go for a walk later on and see it all for yourself.'

She took a sideways glance at her new guest, and thought that a few good days by the sea wouldn't come amiss. Miss Duff was a peelie-wallie young woman, she thought privately, without much colour to her, and not really very smart for a city girl. She had an old-fashioned look about her for a young woman of her age, but Beattie Sinclair decided she'd be the last to complain about that!

'Are most of the men fishermen?' Jenny was asking, turning for a last look at the pretty cottages which made up most of Lethansea. It would be from these homes that most of her pupils would come.

'Some are from the factory further down the coast. That's the alginate works, you see.'

'Alginate?'

Mrs. Sinclair thought that for a teacher Miss Duff was a bit on the ignorant side. However, no doubt she was only supposed to teach writing and sums.

'It's a seaweed factory,' she explained, with a broad attempt at accuracy.

'Of course,' said Jenny, remembering.

'Take your jacket off and we'll leave your cases in your room. You can have a wash, if you like, while I infuse the tea. Mr. Maxwell works there.'

'Works there?'

Jenny wasn't yet used to Beattie Sinclair's abrupt change of subject.

'Lives in that house further up the

road with his mother. She's quite a lady, is Mrs. Maxwell, and Mr. Robin's got a head on his shoulders. Letters after his name, though I forget what they are, but he looks at things in bottles at the factory, and tests it all, I believe. Mrs. Maxwell explained it all to me once. I give her a wee hand in the house now and again. I'll pour your tea, if you won't be a minute.'

Jenny was two minutes, but she sat down to eat with enjoyment.

'I think I'm going to love it here at Lethansea,' she confided happily. 'I hope Miss McLean has a lovely time in Canada. I feel most grateful to her for making this opportunity for me.'

'Aye.'

For once Mrs. Sinclair was non-committal, and the smile left Jenny's face. It looked as though she had put her foot in it somewhere, but she couldn't think where.

'I have about a week to spare before school starts again,' she said, changing the subject. 'I thought I'd come early, though, and get used to Lethansea before I meet the children. It's a big change for me.'

Beattie Sinclair brightened.

'I'm very glad you did,' she said sincerely. 'I heard you'd been having your troubles . . . '

She broke off and coloured a little.

'Lethansea is a wee place, Miss Duff,' she explained carefully. 'News gets round fast, and Mrs. Paterson, the headmaster's wife, told me that you'd just lost your mother. It's sad for a young lady like you to be left on your own, but you'll find plenty of folks here willing to stop you feeling lonely. That is, if you don't mind being one of the community.'

Jenny felt warmed by the older woman's words. It would be wonderful to feel that she belonged somewhere, even if it was only for two terms. Briefly she thought about Charles, who was quite confident that she would be glad to come back to him after her work was finished here.

'I . . . I'll be glad to be one of the community, Mrs. Sinclair,' she said, rather huskily.

'That's fine,' the older woman beamed, 'and just call me Beattie. Everybody does in Lethansea.'

'Beattie,' smiled Jenny. 'My first name is Jenny.'

'Oh, but you'll be Miss Duff to me,' Beattie told her firmly. 'You're the teacher.'

'Oh,' said Jenny.

There was a short silence, then Beattie looked out of the window.

'If you don't feel too tired, why don't you take a walk along the sea-front while I clear away? You'll be wanting to your bed early, and a wee walk will help you to sleep.'

'That's a fine idea,' acknowledged Jenny gratefully, although it wouldn't be her normal bedtime for an hour or two yet.

She enjoyed her walk, picking her way among boulders, and smiling to the few people she met, some with small children and others out exercising their dogs. They all greeted her pleasantly, and Jenny felt that somehow they knew, or guessed, that she was the new teacher.

She walked out along the small natural harbour, gazing down into fishing boats and wondering why the fishermen weren't all swept into the sea in rough weather. She looked at a lamp set in the harbour wall, and thought that someone was probably responsible for lighting it on dark nights to guide in the boats.

The cool breeze whipped her hair around her cheeks, and her skirts around her knees, and she suddenly felt giddy as she walked along the narrow wall and looked down at the seaweed moving, almost with a life of its own, as the sea washed over it.

Was this the seaweed which the factory 'manufactured'? wondered Jenny. Was this what Robin Maxwell tested in 'wee bottles'?

Jenny had no head for heights, even

small ones, and decided to turn back and make for her new home, oddly named Howlett Cottage. There was a great deal more to investigate, but suddenly she felt tired, and hampered by her clothes and rather long hair.

She hadn't bothered about clothing since long before her mother died, but now she began to realise that she only had herself to consider and she had been very neglectful over her own appearance during the past year or two.

'Maybe I could go into Ayr or Girvan and do some shopping,' she decided, as her shoes again sank into the mossy soil.

Maybe she could even have her hair cut. Her mother had always liked it long, but Jenny had often thought she had too much hair for her small pale face.

Whatever she did, she could hardly ruin any beauty since there wasn't much to ruin, she decided, catching a glimpse of herself reflected in a window. She would aim for comfort with neatness and never mind about trying to make the most of her looks when she hadn't any idea how to go about it.

A car passed her near Howlett Cottage, and pulled up outside The Whins, where the Maxwells lived, and Jenny looked at the tall man who got out of the car and turned to stare back at her. He was a large young man with dark chestnut-coloured hair, his skin well sprinkled with freckles.

'Hello,' he grinned, walking towards her. 'I expect you're the new teacher, Miss Duff. I'm Robin Maxwell.'

He held out a hand and Jenny shook it, feeling shy and very conscious of her dowdy, windblown appearance.

'Mrs . . . Beattie . . . told me about you, Mr . . . Mr. Maxwell,' she stammered. 'You manufacture seaweed.'

'I'd be the clever one to do that,' he returned with a laugh, 'and I would have thought there was plenty about without having to manufacture it.'

Jenny grinned.

'You must come to the Works some time, Miss Duff,' Robin Maxwell told her. 'We can't have you teaching the wee ones if there are gaps in your own education.'

Jenny withdrew a little into her shell. The words had been lightly spoken, but Robin Maxwell's appraising eyes had swept over her, and were obviously not terribly impressed with what he saw.

'Thank you, Mr. Maxwell,' she said, with dignity. 'There are gaps in my education, but I'm always willing to learn. Good afternoon.'

'Good evening,' he nodded. 'It's after nine o'clock. I was working late tonight.'

How time had flown, thought Jenny, as she pushed open the small wooden gate, and opened the cottage door after a small knock. Beattie had told her she must just open the door and walk in, since it was her home, too. She had been out on the sea-front for much longer than she'd supposed.

'I saw you talking to Mr. Maxwell,' Beattie informed her. 'He'll be taking you round the factory, no doubt.'

'He . . . he offered,' Jenny agreed, wondering what sort of ears Beattie had to hear all that.

'I thought so,' the older woman told her. 'He fair lives for that place, and enjoys showing it off.'

For some reason Jenny felt slightly deflated. She had allowed herself to believe, for a moment, that Robin Maxwell was doing something special by offering to show her round. But now Beattie was telling her that it was something he did for most people.

Anyway, why think so much about Robin Maxwell? He'd only been polite to the new teacher, who was now his next door neighbour, if temporarily. As a person he hadn't seen her at all.

In spite of herself, that rankled a little to Jenny.

* * *

27

Over the next few days, Jenny enjoyed settling in. Adam Paterson and his wife, Jean, invited her to the schoolhouse for tea, and she listened eagerly to information about the small school and the assortment of parents whom Adam seemed to know intimately.

'We've one or two clever ones,' he told Jenny, 'one or two who will go far, and the others who are only waiting to get through Secondary Modern before taking up labouring jobs. You can see the pattern even in Primary School.'

Jenny nodded. She'd seen the pattern before.

'You'll have wee Steven McLean in your class, though, and I hope you'll be able to make something of him. I never thought it was a good idea for Beryl to teach her own nephew. He's a nice wee lad, and I'm sure he has a good brain, but he's very nervous, poor child. I . . . I sometimes wonder if there isn't discord in that house. Poor Beryl looked ready for her break in Canada before she left.'

Jenny was interested.

'Then she's a local girl?' she asked, 'with relatives still here?'

Adam grinned.

'I keep forgetting you're a stranger,' he told her. 'Yes, they were a fine family once, and have owned Westerhouse, that biggish white house just south of the village, for years. Andrew McLean, Beryl's father, had a good business in Ayr, coach-building. It's only a small place, but he had a good reputation. He died suddenly of a heart attack while the three children were in their teens. Beryl, in fact, was only twelve, but Neil was nearly twenty. Mrs. McLean struggled on for a few years, then she went, too. She was a fine woman, was Elizabeth Manson.'

'Oh, how sad,' said Jenny, feeling sympathy for the family. She knew what it felt like to be on her own, though Beryl, at least, had a brother and sister.

'Yes,' nodded Adam, filling his pipe. 'Nancy married and went off to Canada, then Neil married Carol Fuller, a girl he met in Edinburgh. She's a beauty all right, but I don't think she and Beryl got on. Beryl was still at home, you see, in Westerhouse and Neil insisted that she should stay there. It was her home.'

'She'd have been better to leave,'. Jean Paterson put in quietly. 'It might have been hard to leave her home, but it would have been better. Two women in one house like that was a mistake, and you can't really blame Carol McLean for wanting the house to herself.'

'Maybe not,' agreed Adam, 'though it would take a funny one not to get on with Beryl. The children love her, and she's such a quiet, gentle sort of girl. I'm glad Nancy sent for her, and I wouldn't be surprised if she doesn't stay over in Canada, even if I can think of at least two young men who'd be sorry!'

His eyes twinkled as they rested on his wife.

'Whatever will Miss Duff think of you, Adam?' she exclaimed indignantly, then turned to smile at Jenny. 'At times he sounds the most awful gossip, but he's really bound up with all his children and sometimes I think he feels like going and living the parents' lives for them, if it would make things easier for the children!'

Adam was laughing heartily.

'There's maybe some truth in that,' he conceded, 'but my own brother, Jim, was a great friend of Beryl's and I've seen her around with Robin Maxwell, too. You'll have met him, I suppose?'

Jenny nodded.

'He's our nearest neighbour, Mr. Paterson.'

'And no doubt he'll be showing you over the alginate works.'

'He's offered to,' said Jenny, a trifle shortly. She was beginning to think she'd turn down that invitation!

'Take him up on it,' advised Adam. 'A few fathers work there, and it should

31

be helpful for you to see round besides the fact that it's a very interesting place.'

Jenny smiled and nodded.

'All right,' she agreed, 'if Mr. Maxwell mentions it again, I'll leap at the chance.'

Walking home, Jenny turned all this new information over in her mind. She was going to have her work cut out for her taking Beryl McLean's place. From all accounts, the young girl seemed to have a unique place in the hearts of pupils and parents in Lethansea. A nice sum of money had been collected round the village and presented to Beryl as a parting gift at a social gathering specially arranged for this purpose.

'How can I follow that?' wondered Jenny, unsure about her own capabilities. She was a good teacher, but she hadn't Beryl's advantage in knowing all her children intimately.

On impulse she turned aside on the main road and strode out briskly.

There would just be time to go and have a look at Westerhouse before going home to Beattie. She'd seen the fine white house once before, but hadn't paid any particular attention to it. Now it drew her like a magnet, with a desire to see the home of the girl whose place she was taking. It must have been difficult for her living in her old home, yet seeing another mistress there. Yet it would be difficult for Carol McLean, too, coming into her new home as a bride, and finding she had also inherited a teenage sister-in-law. And what about Neil McLean, torn between the two? No wonder the wee boy, Steven, was nervous. She would have to be specially patient with him, decided Jenny.

Now the lovely white house hove in sight, and Jenny paused, standing on a grassy bank to gaze up at it. It had been built in a sheltered area, with large windows to give fine views of the sea, and must be costly to keep up.

Jenny looked at the house curiously,

deciding that it was very beautiful, and no wonder Beryl hadn't wanted to leave it while she worked in Lethansea. She must be a very special sort of girl to hold the love and affection of so many people.

Even Robin Maxwell? From what Mr. Paterson had said it looked as though they were very special friends, and no doubt he was missing her, even if it was only for a few months. Perhaps he wouldn't take kindly to seeing her there, in Beryl's place.

Jenny kicked at the stones by the side of the road as she walked back home. It was a habit from childhood when her thoughts were busy elsewhere, and she pulled herself up with a small laugh. Why worry about Beryl McLean, who was no doubt enjoying a wonderful experience, and an exciting change of scene?

Her thoughts turned to other things as she reached Howlett Cottage and walked round to the back door. It was becoming more and more like her own home, and she was growing very fond of Beattie.

'Did you have a nice time?' the older woman beamed as she walked in. 'Mrs. Paterson makes people very welcome, and the schoolmaster is very well liked. You should get on with them fine, Miss Duff. Did you get plenty to eat, or will I make you something extra for supper? I've just set the wee table with one or two egg sandwiches and scones.'

'Oh, Beattie, I couldn't manage another bite!'

'Not even an egg sandwich?'

'Well . . .'

Jenny managed the egg sandwiches.

★ ★ ★

Next morning Beattie picked up the mail and brought it in triumph to the breakfast table.

'Another letter from Glasgow for you, Miss Duff,' she said with a broad smile. 'Somebody's missing you a lot.'

Jenny coloured and took Charles'

letter, glancing up at Beattie. She knew the older woman was dying to know more about her private life, and that it was more from genuine, kindly interest than sheer nosiness. Nevertheless she didn't feel capable of explaining about Charles in a way which would satisfy that curiosity.

'He's just a friend, Beattie,' she said, with a small smile.

'Och well, it's good to have friends,' Beattie acknowledged. 'You must ask him to visit you some time. I love visitors, so don't be late about asking anybody you fancy, Miss Duff. They'll aye get a welcome from me.'

'You're very kind, Beattie.'

Jenny was genuinely grateful to her landlady, and felt again the relief and happiness of having somewhere comfortable to stay. She had been very lonely after her mother died, but now it was a great comfort to have Beattie to talk to.

'I'm going into Ayr today,' she confided. 'I thought I'd buy a new suit, and perhaps some skirts and blouses for the start of term. I need to have my hair cut, too.'

'I'm very glad to hear it,' Beattie told her, 'not that it's any of my business, but I like to see young girls make the most of themselves. There aren't any plain girls these days, not like there were in my day. At least, not . . .'

'Not when they've gone to a little bit of trouble,' finished Jenny, laughing. 'I'm afraid I'd let myself get into a rut, Beattie.'

'You had too much to do, Miss Duff. It's high time you had somebody to look after you.'

Beattie plumped up cushions vigorously. She was growing fond of the new schoolteacher, and resolved to bring the roses back into her cheeks before she left Lethansea. Now she saw Miss Duff away, happily, glad that the girl was beginning to show more interest in herself.

Jenny had a thoroughly enjoyable day in Ayr, finding some delightful shops which sold her just what she wanted. She thought Beattie would approve of the new clothes she had bought, which were modern without being too outlandish.

Her visit to the hairdresser's, however, proved rather disappointing. She had decided that a short, simple hairstyle would be the most practical for her new job, and saw her long heavy hair fall to the floor without too much regret.

But her face was still too pale and thin for the short hairstyle, and the cheekbones seemed to stand out more prominently than ever.

'I'll just have to be Beattie's first plain young woman,' she told herself humorously. 'At least it's easy to manage now.'

Making for the bus station, her parcels large and cumbersome, Jenny stood on the pavement to allow traffic to pass, and was surprised and slightly taken aback when a large dark blue car slid to a halt.

'Going home, Miss Duff?'

Robin Maxwell peered at her from the driving seat, and Jenny nodded, smiling shyly.

'Get in then, quickly,' he said, a trifle impatiently. 'This isn't a good place to stop. Just heave your parcels into the back of the car.'

She did so, and slid into the passenger seat, and he drove away quickly.

'Done all your shopping?' he asked, glancing at her. 'Got your hair cut, too, I see. You look . . .'

'I know. Like a skinned rabbit,' she finished ruefully, and he grinned.

'Now I wouldn't have put it like that, Miss Duff.'

'No, you'd have been polite, but it would have meant the same in the end.'

This time he laughed heartily.

'And are you settled down now before starting to teach all our little ones? I admire anyone who takes it upon themselves to train young minds.'

Like Beryl McLean? wondered Jenny, remembering what Adam Paterson had told her.

'It's a job I love,' she told him simply.

'It's a fine thing to love your work,' he observed. 'As a matter of fact . . . '

'If you're going to renew your invitation to visit your alginate works, then I accept,' she said promptly, and again he laughed.

'Well . . .'

'I understand you enjoy showing people round.'

This time the smile left his eyes.

'Now we must get our facts right, Miss Duff. I'm very proud of our factory, one of the few in the world, but I only show people round who realise it's an honour and a privilege. Some of our competitors would give a great deal to be taken round the plant. The doors aren't thrown open to everybody, you know.'

Jenny's cheeks coloured and she looked chastened.

'I'm sorry, I didn't know. I . . . I'd still like to come, if I may.'

'Then we'll make it tomorrow, if that suits you.'

They had left Ayr behind, and Robin was driving down the coast road with skill and care.

'How beautiful it all is,' she said appreciatively. 'I've explored quite a few places already.'

'Culzean Castle?'

'Oh yes. I thought it was magnificent.'

'Crossraguel Abbey, near Maybole?'

This time she shook her head.

'No. At least, not yet. I . . . I hadn't heard about it.'

'I can see you need a guide, Miss Duff. I'll be happy to offer my services now and again.'

Jenny was surprised and rather touched. Robin Maxwell must be a busy man, and she had no illusions about any desire he might have for her company. Then she remembered that Beryl McLean was now in Canada, and no doubt he was feeling rather lonely.

Perhaps he felt that Beryl would not be at all jealous of a Plain Jane like herself!

'It's very kind of you,' she acknowledged quietly, and again he glanced at her.

'Do I detect lack of enthusiasm?' he inquired, and again the warm colour stole into her cheeks.

'No, of course not. I'm just grateful that you're offering to spare the time.'

This time his look was frankly curious.

'I'll be delighted to spare the time, Miss Duff,' he assured her, turning the car down the small narrow road which led to their respective homes.

'Come out to the Works at about half-past two tomorrow. I've already got permission from our general manager. I'll look out for you then.'

'Thank you. Cheerio, Mr. Maxwell.'

'Till tomorrow, Miss Duff.'

If Beattie was disappointed that Miss Duff hadn't exactly turned into a swan, she didn't show it. Instead she admired the new purchases in a very satisfactory way.

'They're very smart, Miss Duff. You should look well in that skirt and blouse.'

Jenny nodded, and smiled rather ruefully.

'Now that Monday's so near, I'm beginning to need a little Dutch courage, Beattie. I was never really nervous at school in Glasgow, but from all I hear of Miss McLean, I'm going to have quite a job taking her place.'

Beattie said nothing for a moment, but again there was a closed look about her face. Surely Beattie wasn't different from everyone else in that she didn't like Beryl McLean? Jenny knew she couldn't question her landlady, but to drop the subject abruptly might indicate that she had guessed something was wrong.

'I believe you gave her a fine send-off party.'

At this Beattie's reserve vanished

and Jenny knew her doubts were very much mistaken when she saw the older woman's softened expression.

'We did indeed,' she said proudly. 'We all worked hard and did it in style. We got up a concert with all the local talent, and all the children took part, right down to the youngest. Och, it was a good night, that. What's more, it got into the papers, and I've kept the photograph. I even went down and got a copy of the newspaper photograph since I'm on it myself . . . in the background, of course, but you can see me as plain as anything.'

Beattie went over to an old-fashioned chest of drawers and rummaged among some papers, to return in triumph with a copy of the newspaper and a large shiny photograph.

'There I am,' she said, pointing to one of the heads in the background. 'What do you think of that?'

Jenny duly admired the photograph which showed Beattie without her usual smile, and her hair freshly set and held stiffly in style, no doubt by the liberal use of hairspray.

Then she turned her attention to the others on the photograph, her gaze becoming riveted on the central figure, a laughing young girl with a sweet, innocent face, wide-set eyes and cloudy dark hair.

Jenny stared, feeling that the face was familiar to her, and trying hard to remember where she had seen the girl before.

'What's wrong, Miss Duff?' Beattie was asking, anxiously.

'Nothing . . . at least, nothing really. Is this Beryl McLean?'

'Aye, that's Miss Beryl.'

Again there was the reserved note in Beattie's voice and she was gazing at Jenny closely.

'Why?'

'I . . . I just thought I'd seen her before, that's all . . . but I can't think where . . .'

'Can you not remember?'

Again there was a hint of controlled

anxiety, and Jenny stared levelly at the older woman.

'Why? Is it important?'

'Oh no,' Beattie denied quickly. 'I was just . . . interested, that was all. It would have been funny if you already knew Miss Beryl. It's a small world, as they say.'

Again Jenny looked at the photograph, smiling at the sight of Adam Paterson and Jean, with Robin Maxwell looking slightly uncomfortable just behind Beryl McLean. There was another, very good-looking dark young man, near Mr. Paterson.

'Who's that?' she asked Beattie.

'That's young Jim Paterson, the schoolmaster's brother. He lives with his parents in Girvan, but he works beside Mr. Maxwell and he's often here visiting his brother. He and Miss Beryl were very pally, too, as was Mr. Maxwell, but she hasn't seemed to settle for any one of them. She's a very popular girl, but sweet and gentle with it, not like her sister-in-law who always wants her own way. From what we've heard, poor Miss Beryl hadn't much of a life in that house . . .'

Beattie broke off. She wasn't really a gossip though her natural love of people made her talk about them more than she cared to at times. Jenny's thoughts were all with the lovely, laughing girl, however.

'Then she didn't decide to live on her own?'

'No,' said Beattie, rather shortly, then softened. It was natural for Miss Duff to be curious about the girl whose job she was taking, if only temporarily.

'She was very fond of wee Steven,' Beattie explained gently. 'He's a nervy wee boy, very highly strung, and Beryl McLean loves him like her own child. She can get him to do anything, even to recite a nice wee poem at the concert. But I've seen him dry up, without a word to say for himself, when his mother brings him round to a fête, or the children's sports day. We rarely see

Mr. Neil. I suppose he'll be kept busy at the Works. It must have been hard for him to take over from his father.'

Jenny nodded, and handed the photo back to Beattie. She'd given up trying to remember where she had seen the girl before.

But that evening, just as she was dropping off to sleep, the laughing face was before her vividly, then she was seeing the laughter drain from the gentle delicate features, and a look of apprehension take its place.

Quite clearly she could see the girl in the restaurant in Glasgow, wearing her neat waitress's uniform, looking at Charles as he complained angrily about poor service.

Jenny found herself wide awake, recalling the scene vividly. But it was only two weeks ago! And Beryl McLean would then have been well on her way to Canada. She must have been mistaken. The girl in the restaurant must have been so like Beryl that they could be twins. That was why the lovely young face had teased her memory. It couldn't possibly have been Beryl McLean she had seen in Glasgow.

Nevertheless, the girl's wide dark eyes seemed to stare into her own, the cloudy dark hair clinging in small wisps to the damp forehead. It was a long time before Jenny could put her from her mind, and drop off to sleep. Tomorrow she would dress up in some of her new clothes, and make her way to the alginate works. The prospect was very pleasing to her, and she felt she was going to enjoy her day.

Jenny fell asleep at last.

3

There was a fresh breeze blowing from the sea the following afternoon when Jenny stepped off the bus outside the alginate works, farther down the coast.

She sniffed the air appreciatively as she walked down to the small factory so charmingly situated close to the sea. There was a tangy smell of seaweed, and the comforting, busy sound of men working efficiently and happily.

Robin Maxwell was looking out for her, and for a brief moment Jenny hoped to see a look of approval on his face when he saw her dressed neatly in her new rich green woollen suit. But Robin was merely satisfied that she was on time, and lost no further time in shepherding her round the plant, which seemed to consist of a great many large vats, vast quantities of water and, at various stages, added chemicals. Jenny looked with fascination at a porridge-like mixture which later became fibrous, and was finally pressed into solids which, in turn, was dried into powder.

'And it all came from seaweed,' said Jenny, marvelling, as she stared at the finished product, beautifully packed in drums. 'Will you be using that seaweed near the harbour at Lethansea?'

'Goodness no,' laughed Robin. 'No, Miss Duff. This is very special seaweed. Our two types have rather grand names, but you might know them best as rock weed and tangle. Haven't you heard of the 'Tangle o' the Isles'?'

'But of course.'

'There you are, then. It's collected in several places, but you'd be mainly interested in North Uist and South Uist. Some time you must go and see the seaweed being collected. Both weeds are used for different purposes.'

'And how do you get it?' asked Jenny, smiling.

'It's brought here aboard puffers to Girvan Harbour.'

Jenny's interest was now well and truly caught as Robin shepherded her into a fine modern building, well planned, with large laboratories and busy offices. She saw the alginate being tested at every stage of its production and a busy team of research chemists working away steadily.

'Are they working out new uses for alginate?' asked Jenny.

'No, they're trying to improve on present methods of producing alginate,' said Robin, with a smile.

'It's used in lots of different things then?'

'Lots of different things. Ice cream and milk desserts, stabilising emulsion paint, thickening detergents . . . it's even used in surgical dressings.'

Jenny paused before leaving the laboratory, her eyes on a tall, dark young man. Surely she'd seen him before . . . but of course, the photograph!

'Isn't that Mr. Paterson's brother?' she asked, as she followed Robin along the corridor.

'Yes.' He turned to her. 'Do you know Jim Paterson?'

'I haven't met him.' She shook her head, and he turned to her again as they descended the stairs.

'Then how . . . ?'

'I saw a photograph. Beattie showed it to me. It was taken at Miss McLean's presentation party before she went to Canada. I asked who everyone was, and Beattie said it was Mr. Paterson's brother.'

Robin nodded, saying nothing for a moment.

'You . . . er . . . haven't heard from Miss McLean yet?' she asked tentatively, and Robin's face took on a closed look.

'No. Why should I?'

'I . . . I thought you were friends.'

'Beattie's an old gossip. Are you going to ask Jim Paterson too? Anyway, why should it matter to you?'

She flushed scarlet. Her thoughts had gone again and again to the young waitress in Glasgow, and above all she wanted reassurance that the girl had nothing to do with Beryl McLean. It would have helped to know that Robin had heard from the girl, and that she was now happy in Canada.

'It doesn't matter to me,' she told him confusedly. 'I was just interested to hear if she arrived safely enough. Surely it's natural to be interested in the girl whose place I'm taking?'

'Well, if she has arrived, she doesn't think me worthy of being informed,' said Robin, and for a moment Jenny wondered if he'd been feeling hurt. Had he been hoping to hear from Beryl, and been disappointed because there had been no letter?

'Canada is a long way off,' she said gently. 'The mail often takes a long time, especially surface mail.'

Robin's brooding eyes considered her thoughtfully, then he smiled.

'You're rather a nice girl, Jenny Duff,' he said unexpectedly. 'Have you enjoyed your visit here then?'

'So much I couldn't begin to tell

you. You must be very proud of it.'

'I am,' he admitted.

'It's a happy place,' she said, looking back when they had almost reached the main road.

'Yes,' he agreed, 'it's a happy place. It's a pity . . . ' He broke off.

'What?'

'Nothing. I was just going to say that it's a pity our private worlds have to intrude sometimes. Perhaps you'd be kind enough to accompany me one evening to a concert, or a show at the theatre? I would enjoy your company.'

Jenny hesitated only for a moment. She knew exactly where she stood with Robin Maxwell, anyway. He was offering her friendship, and that suited her, decided Jenny as she accepted and bade him farewell. Yet there was a deep feeling of disquiet in her as she waited for her bus. She had only known Robin Maxwell for a week or two, yet already she could feel the strength of his personality intruding into her life. She reminded herself that it was Beryl McLean who was important to him, and began to wonder about Jim Paterson. Had he heard from Beryl? she wondered. Or was Jim Paterson, too, waiting longingly for a letter which hadn't yet arrived?

The bus came and Jenny climbed aboard, looking out at the darkening sea as clouds blew up and blocked out the sun. She thought of the tangle, the sea tangle, and she felt that she herself seemed to be becoming involved in a different sort of tangle.

Why couldn't she forget about Beryl McLean, a girl she hadn't even met? Why couldn't she just concentrate on the job she had come to do, and try to pass her two terms in Lethansea quietly, efficiently and happily?

Yet she knew she wasn't the type of person to stand aloof in a community. She loved people, and couldn't help becoming bound up in their lives. Already she was looking forward to seeing Beattie's cheery face when she walked in the door, and to hearing her talk happily about the doings of friends and neighbours.

And she was also looking forward to going out again with Robin Maxwell. He must have enjoyed her company or he wouldn't have asked her, she thought with a small stab of pleasure.

The sun escaped from behind the clouds and drenched Lethansea in a shower of glory. The white walls of Howlett Cottage sparkled, and the roses were encouraged to fill the air with perfume.

Jenny, too, was encouraged to hop and skip up the front path. She felt better than she had done for months, and the breeze had whipped colour into her cheeks.

Beattie thought that Miss Duff was beginning to look quite bonny. A wee bit filling out, and it would make quite a difference to her.

'Did you have a good day,' she asked, 'seeing all that seaweed being manufactured?'

'Beattie, I had a lovely day,' Jenny told her. 'Isn't Lethansea a lovely place?'

Beattie agreed that it was.

* * *

Jenny's first week as the new teacher at Lethansea Primary School was absorbing but uneventful. The village was small and there were few pupils, but Jenny found her children intelligent and quick to learn. They could also become quickly bored, and she had to keep on her toes to stay ahead of them.

She began to know quite a lot about her small charges and their background, and to recognise the ones who needed a firm hand, and the quieter children who could make such good progress with encouragement.

Young Steven McLean was one of the quiet ones, accepting her warily, and very slow to respond to her efforts to win his trust and affection, if possible.

Jenny often went home at night tired with her efforts, but sympathising with the little boy. He probably missed his Aunt Beryl very much indeed, and was bewildered by her disappearance out of his life, even if the reason had been carefully explained to him. He would have looked askance at anyone taking her place, and Jenny resolved to be very patient with the child. She had been told he was very intelligent, but so far he had shown little evidence of this in his wooden response to her efforts.

'Are you finding it hard going at first?' Adam Paterson asked sympathetically.

'A little.'

'Take it easy, then. They'll soon get used to you and begin to accept you. They've known Beryl all their lives, don't forget.'

'I know,' said Jenny, rather dismally.

'Being a stranger has its advantages, too,' said Adam gently.

Now and again she had stumbled a little and found she wasn't doing things as Miss McLean did them.

'I'm not worried about any of the children,' she assured Adam. 'I feel confident I can handle them once I get to know them better, but wee Steven is rather different.'

'Doesn't he do what he's told?'

She was silent for a while.

'No, it's not that. In fact, it's the opposite. I think I'd welcome a little bit of mischief, but he's really rather wooden, and I feel that a boy like him should be like a piece of quicksilver. He looks as though the fairies have stolen him away, and left a small block of wood in his place.'

'Is he that bad? I'd better have a word with him . . . '

'No, I'm exaggerating. Don't take any notice of me. I've already decided the little boy is only acting naturally under the circumstances. How is Miss McLean, by the way?'

'I haven't heard personally,' Adam admitted, 'which isn't really like her. She's a very thoughtful young woman, but I expect she's caught up in a whirlwind. I visited America a couple of years back, and I'm only just getting my breath back now!'

He grinned, but Jenny's answering smile was wavery. So nobody had heard from Beryl McLean. Against her will her thoughts went back again to that girl in the restaurant. She had tried hard not to think it was the same girl, but every instinct was telling her that it was. She had been the girl in Beattie's photograph all right.

But why? Why should Beryl McLean say she was going to Canada to stay with her sister, get leave of absence for two terms, accept a generous gift at a farewell party, then quietly hide herself away in Glasgow? And why should she get herself a job serving as a waitress when she was a trained schoolteacher?

Jenny's head began to ache as questions chased each other in and out of her mind. Soon she would have to find an excuse to go back to Glasgow and visit that restaurant again. She would have to get hold of that girl, and ask her if she really was Beryl McLean, and settle the matter in her own mind.

' . . . spread the news,' Adam Paterson was saying.

'I'm sorry . . . I didn't quite catch,' said Jenny guiltily.

'I said maybe Beryl's relying on her brother Neil to spread the news round that she's fairly enjoying herself.'

'Oh . . . is she? Then he's heard, then?'

Adam looked at her curiously, and she was made aware of the eagerness in her voice and drew back a little.

'I mean . . . I was just wondering . . .'

'It's natural, I expect, with you taking her place. Yes, Jean saw Neil yesterday and asked after Beryl. He says she's fine and having a wonderful time.'

'I see. I am glad.'

Relief made Jenny bubble with laughter, and she was glad Mr. Paterson hadn't been able to read her thoughts. He would have thought her quite mad, confusing a young waitress in Glasgow with Miss McLean, on the strength of a photograph! Thank goodness the matter was now settled and she could stop worrying about it.

★ ★ ★

'My brother Jim saw you going round the alginate works,' said Adam as they parted outside his cottage. 'Robin Maxwell offered to take you round, then? I was glad to hear you'd taken him up on it. If he hadn't, I'd have prodded Jim into getting the necessary permission from the general manager.'

'I enjoyed it,' Jenny told him. 'You were quite right, and I'm very glad I had the opportunity.'

Adam nodded, his gentle brown eyes regarding her thoughtfully.

'Jim would like to make your acquaintance, so Jean and I wondered if you were free on Sunday evening, and she'll invite both of you to supper.'

Jenny's eyes lit up with pleasure.

'That's very nice of you both. Of

course I'd love to come and meet your brother. I . . . I rather think I noticed him in the laboratory . . . '

'But you haven't met him yet, have you?'

Again she coloured and smiled.

'No, but Beattie showed me a photograph of you all. I . . . er . . . I remembered.'

There was a decided twinkle in Adam's eyes.

'I see. Sunday night, then, Jenny. Seven-thirty, if that suits.'

'It suits fine.'

It was nice to have something to look forward to, decided Jenny, as she walked home. She thought again about the tall dark young man who was Adam Paterson's brother. It would be very interesting to meet him, too. From what she could gather, although he and Robin Maxwell had been rivals for Beryl McLean, they seemed to be good friends as well as colleagues.

Jenny liked that. It showed that they were worthy people in her eyes, able to have a well-balanced attitude towards each other. She already knew Robin Maxwell, and had decided he was very worthwhile. Now she wondered what Jim Paterson would be like.

She would look forward to Sunday, and she would wear that lovely new cream silk dress. Of all her recent purchases, she liked that best.

4

On Saturday Jenny received one of her letters from Charles, but this one was different.

'It seems a long time since you left Glasgow,' he wrote, 'and you don't really tell me anything about Lethansea except that it's a nice place and you've settled down. I've a feeling you'd say that anyway, Jenny, since you're only there for a few months. But there's no need to stick it out for the sake of false pride.

'Anyway, I've decided to come and see for myself, and I'll catch the morning train to Ayr on Saturday. There'll be no need to meet me. I can find my own way to your lodgings quite easily. I'm very much looking forward to seeing you again, and hope you feel the same way. I walked round to your home last night, but the tenants seem to be keeping the place in order. I could find no fault with it.'

Jenny looked at the envelope which bore a four-penny stamp, and saw that the letter had been in the post for three days. He might have sent it first class, she thought crossly, and given her time to prepare for his visit.

Yet what did she need to prepare? Nothing really.

'Er . . . my friend from Glasgow would like to come and see me today. Is that all right, Beattie?'

Beattie appeared from the kitchen, beaming with pleasure.

'Of course, that'll be fine, Miss Duff. I could get some boiled ham from the wee shop and we've plenty of salad stuff. Would he eat a nice fresh salad?'

'I'm sure he would,' Jenny smiled, then was surprised to find she didn't really know Charles tastes very well. But he could like the salad or lump it, she told herself. A few hours' notice was too short to pander to tastes.

She wasn't really looking forward to seeing Charles, she realised, looking at herself honestly. She was settling down well, and didn't want to be unsettled in any way, and he had a knack of picking on things which could worry her. Then she felt ashamed of her ungraciousness, and began to make plans to welcome him. She would take him for a walk round the village, and show him the school, then perhaps there would be time to go and see Culzean Castle. Charles might enjoy that.

It was just shortly after lunch when he rang the doorbell, and Jenny went to let him in and introduce him to Beattie.

'I'm very pleased to meet you, Mr. Cairns,' the older woman beamed. 'Any friend o' Miss Duff's is most welcome. Will I make you a quick meal? We didn't know what time you'd arrive . . . '

'No need for that,' Charles assured her. 'I had my lunch in Ayr.' He turned to Jenny. 'You look different.

68

What have you done to your hair?'

'Had it cut,' she said briefly.

Charles didn't look at all approving, but she quickly got him talking about their school in Glasgow, and Beattie discreetly left them alone.

'I thought we'd take a walk round the village,' Jenny suggested brightly, after Charles had had a rest.

'Very well. I hope it isn't muddy, though, Jenny. I'm wearing my best clothes.'

She had seen that already, noting his rather stiff grey suit and very new brown shoes.

'I . . . I don't think so, Charles. We'll just be careful.'

As they walked along she pointed out places which had seemed breathtakingly lovely to her, but under Charles' rather critical eyes, they became more ordinary and not really remarkable at all. Even the school seemed very small and grey.

'I'm not happy about you here, Jenny,' said Charles at last. 'I don't really think it's doing you any good. I mean, there's nothing here for a girl like you. I was sure of that, so I decided to come and talk over our future . . . '

'I thought we'd go on to Culzean Castle,' said Jenny quickly, 'and here's a bus now, though it's only a short ride. Wouldn't you like to do that, Charles?'

'Oh, all right,' he agreed, a trifle huffily.

But the beautiful castle with the lovely Adam architecture only kept Charles from having his say for a limited period. He couldn't fail to enjoy what he saw, and for a time Jenny was happy in his company. She had known Charles a long time, and there was something comfortable about old friends, though she couldn't relax completely in his company, knowing that the time must come when she would again have to disappoint him.

As they leaned over the wall and looked down at the sea which was shrouded in mist, Charles reached over and took her hand.

'Haven't you had time to think, Jenny?' he asked, quite gently. 'Don't you think you'd be happier back home as my wife?'

'You know I couldn't come back just now, Charles,' she pointed out. 'I've promised to stay here for two terms and I must keep that promise.'

'Surely it wouldn't be impossible to replace you.'

'It wouldn't be good for the children to be upset again, especially for someone like little Steven McLean.'

'Who's he?'

'Miss McLean's nephew. She's the young teacher whose place I'm taking. Her nephew is a pupil at the school.'

Charles frowned.

'Surely you don't have to worry about him. Hasn't he got parents?'

'Yes, but . . . '

'There you are, then. I'm trying to save you worry, Jenny, and give you my protection.' He grew suddenly rather stiff. 'Obviously it's being misplaced.'

'Oh no, Charles! I . . . I do appreciate that you . . . you're doing me an honour.'

She was probably lucky, she thought ruefully, to have anyone take an interest in her at all, and she couldn't help suspecting that Charles felt exactly the same.

'Well?' he asked. 'I've already asked you to marry me, though I realise you needed time to consider. Now I'm asking you again, Jenny.'

She felt cold suddenly, looking down into the mist. It was as though her own life was shrouded in that mist, because she knew that sooner or later she would have to leave Lethansea, and go back to Glasgow.

What would be there for her if she put Charles out of her life? The future seemed like this thickening cloud and she could hear the gulls crying and the sea surging on the cliffs below.

She didn't want to leave Lethansea, ever, and didn't want to be reminded of a time when it would all be gone from her, and the call of the sea would only be heard in her memory.

'I don't want to think about marriage just now, Charles,' she said uneasily. 'I can't leave Lethansea until I've fulfilled my duties here. I'm sorry.'

'Very well, Jenny.' Charles' voice was cold, and he turned away stiffly. 'I shall catch the next bus for Ayr. I hope it connects with a suitable train.'

'Oh, but Beattie is preparing tea for us,' she protested. 'She'll be very disappointed. You can't just go and leave it all, just like that.'

'I wasn't aware that I'd made any special arrangements with Mrs. Sinclair.'

Jenny bit back an angry reply. She could see that Charles looked upset, and realised that perhaps it would be better for him to go now.

'There might not be a bus,' she said, looking at her watch. 'We might have to wait a little.'

A few moments later a car drew up

at the gates of the Castle, and Robin Maxwell leaned over and wound down the window.

'Going into Ayr, Jenny? Can I give you both a lift?'

Jenny hesitated a moment, looking up at Charles, but already he was accepting politely, and opening the car door for Jenny.

'This is Mr. Maxwell,' she introduced them, 'our next-door neighbour. Robin, this is Charles Cairns, an old friend from Glasgow.'

'Beattie said you'd arrived, Mr. Cairns,' said Robin, after they had greeted each other. 'Are you having to leave sooner than you expected?'

It was so near the mark that neither Jenny nor Charles answered for a moment.

'Yes,' they both said at last, and lapsed into uncomfortable silence.

'You'll have to come another time,' Robin told him conversationally. 'I'm sure we could find plenty to interest you.'

'The tangle o' the Isles?' asked Jenny, rather teasingly.

'Not to everyone's taste,' said Robin, and quickly changed the subject. 'Is it the station, then, Mr. Cairns? Are you going home by train?'

'Yes, thank you,' Charles acknowledged. 'I'm most grateful for the lift.'

'I'll be half an hour in Ayr, Jenny. I'll come back and pick you up here.'

Robin didn't wait to take no for an answer, and both Jenny and Charles stood back as the car sped away.

'You seem to have lost no time in forming friendships,' said Charles, a trifle jealously. 'You say Maxwell's a neighbour? You should be careful, though, Jenny, not to be too hasty about forming relationships with people.'

'Robin Maxwell is a degreed chemist with Alginate Industries,' said Jenny, with a lift of her chin. 'He's a fine man, and anyone would be proud to be his friend.'

Happily the train was due to leave shortly and there was no more time for argument. Jenny followed Charles on to the platform, and looked at him with troubled eyes. The visit had not been a success, and she hated to part bad friends with him for the sake of the years they had known one another.

'I'm sorry, Charles,' she said quietly. 'You haven't enjoyed it much, have you?'

The answer surprised and rather shook her, for Charles suddenly turned and pulled her into his arms, kissing her clumsily but heartily.

'I'll see you again, Jenny,' he told her firmly.

Jenny felt confused and sought to change the subject, wishing that the train would start to move.

'Oh, Charles!' she said hurriedly, 'were you ever back at that restaurant we went to? Have you noticed if that young waitress is still there . . . the new one with dark hair?'

Charles looked astonished at her question.

'Of course not! Go back there to see

if they've kept on that inefficient girl? You do wonder odd things at times, Jenny.'

The train jolted, then gathered speed, and she waved until it turned the bend, then walked back thoughtfully to the station entrance. It hadn't been the best of days, and she felt very confused with regard to Charles.

She was still thinking about him when Robin's blue car again swept in front of the station entrance, and he waved for her to get in the car.

'Thanks, Robin,' she said, as she climbed in.

They were both silent as Robin negotiated the car out of Ayr, and along the coast road.

'Is . . . er . . . Mr. Cairns a very old friend?' Robin asked at last.

'He was a colleague of mine in Glasgow,' she told him briefly.

'I see,' said Robin, but his tone of voice said that he was curious about Charles Cairns, and Jenny didn't feel like talking at the moment. Now that the train had gone, she felt rather upset and wondered again if she had done the right thing in turning down Charles' proposal.

She didn't think she loved him, but she had never been in love, so perhaps what she felt for Charles would have developed into the right kind of love for marriage.

Jenny had seen other people in love, girls at University, and other teachers who had left to get married. In some cases it seemed a very up-and-down affair, with rapturous faces one day, and decidedly long ones the next. Perhaps her long familiar association with Charles was a much more lasting basis for marriage than some quick, surging emotion which would burn itself out just as quickly.

Besides, she ought to be grateful that somebody did want to share her life, since she was hardly a raving beauty. The trouble was, she suspected, Charles thought so, too!

'You're very quiet, Jenny.'

Robin's voice broke into her thoughts.

'Sorry,' she apologised. 'I was only thinking something out.'

'Would it help to talk about it?' he asked gently.

'That's nice of you,' she smiled, 'but I don't think so. It's a very personal problem.'

'I see,' he said again, then decided to change the subject.

'The weather's settled at the moment, so I wondered if you'd like a wee run out tomorrow afternoon? We could go down to Ballantrae, and perhaps on to Stranraer, or if you like we could go north to Troon or Largs.'

'Oh, I am sorry,' said Jenny, disappointed, because the prospect of a run out with Robin was distinctly attractive. 'Mr. Paterson has asked me to tea to meet his brother Jim.'

Robin was silent for a moment.

'I hope you have a nice evening.' He laughed ruefully. 'I forgot that you're bound to get plenty of invitations, and Jim Paterson's a fine chap. You'll like him.'

There was a slightly strained note in his voice, however, and Jenny was reminded of the supposed rivalry between him and Jim. It would be interesting to meet Jim, and to wonder a little which one of the two was most likely to win Beryl McLean. Perhaps she had been asked to make up her mind while she was away.

'How about next Saturday, then?' pursued Robin. 'Are you free then?'

'I am,' laughed Jenny.

'I'll pick you up at two-thirty, then. Here we are . . . home again . . . I'll see you later, Jenny.'

'Thanks for the lift,' she told him, climbing out of the car and catching sight of Beattie at the window.

With a sinking heart she suddenly realised she was going to have some explaining to do as to why Charles wasn't here to eat his boiled ham and salad!

Beattie was disappointed. Jenny felt very guilty when she looked at the table which had been tastefully set for tea.

'I'm sorry,' she said apologetically. 'Charles . . . Charles found he had to go back to Glasgow earlier than he expected. I . . . I should have let you know, Beattie.'

The older woman couldn't help looking slightly huffed, and Jenny bit her lip.

'We had a disagreement about something,' she admitted.

'Oh, I see.'

'But I'm starving, and if you haven't had your own tea, couldn't we have it together? It all looks so tempting.'

Beattie thawed, and after a moment's hesitation she agreed to Jenny's suggestion.

'I'll just pour out the tea, then, Miss Duff. I hope the disagreement . . . er . . . wasn't serious.'

Jenny's eyes were sad for a moment.

'I . . . I don't think so,' she said.

But she felt that one of the doors of her life was beginning to close. She was glad Beattie was sharing her meal, or her appetite might have been poor today, but now she listened happily to all the doings of the neighbourhood, and began to feel quite a lot better.

'I hear that young Mrs. McLean has been throwing her weight about, wanting to organise the Christmas Social,' Beattie told her.

'What's the Christmas Social?'

'Och, it's a sort of entertainment we get up each year at Christmas to help the over-sixties in the neighbourhood. Usually we have a sale of work, followed by a concert or a dance. We'd all voted for a concert this year, since it was a dance last time. But Mrs. McLean says we should have a dance again . . . she's dancing mad, that one . . . and the Women's Fellowship have had a rare old argument over it. Mrs. Maxwell's all huffed because she arranges the concert, you see?'

Jenny didn't really see too well.

'But why does Mrs. McLean want to have it altered?'

'Because Miss Beryl won't be here, and she always plays the piano for the concert and trains up the wee ones to do a turn, too. I don't suppose you play the piano, Miss Duff?'

Jenny didn't quite know what to say. She played a little, enough to help out with teaching her children singing, but she was hardly the sort of pianist Beattie must have in mind.

'Only a very little,' she admitted.

The older woman's eyes lit up.

'Well then, you'll maybe be able to take it on. Mrs. Maxwell said she was going to ask you . . . '

'Oh no, please,' said Jenny, in horror. 'I'm not that good, Beattie. I could never play a lot of accompaniments.'

'I think it would be just simple stuff, Miss Duff,' said Beattie encouragingly. 'We don't go in for anything fancy. I bet you'd manage to do it fine.' She eyed Jenny with pleasure. 'It's wonderful the way you are managing to step in for Miss Beryl. I think we've all been very lucky you've come here. Miss Beryl . . . '

Beattie broke off and again there was a closed look about her face, as though she'd remembered something.

'Would you like another cup of tea?' she asked, rather quickly.

'No, thank you. It's been a lovely meal.' She smiled wryly. 'Charles should have stayed for it.'

Yet she was relieved now that he hadn't. She helped Beattie with the washing up, and decided to go to bed early. The sea air had made her tired, and she was able to sleep better at nights than she had done for years.

In addition, it was tanning her skin a pale golden brown which made her eyes look almost golden and gave bright lights to her brown hair.

The same thought must have occurred to Beattie as she watched Jenny hang out the tea-towel.

'You're growing quite bonny, Miss

Duff,' she said with satisfaction. 'Your face has filled out and it suits you.'

Jenny laughed and coloured a little.

'Thank you, Beattie. I'm afraid I've a long way to go before I can be called handsome.'

'Handsome is as handsome does,' Beattie quoted heavily. 'I'm right glad to have you here for company. Sometimes the winter can be long when you're by yourself.'

'I know,' said Jenny softly. 'You must miss your husband, Beattie. Have you no relatives living nearby?'

'I've a sister in Girvan with a husband and three young sons. The eldest . . .' Beattie paused, 'the eldest is working in a big office in Glasgow. He's in digs there . . .'

'Does he like it?' asked Jenny.

'Oh, aye.'

There was an odd note in Beattie's voice again, and suddenly she turned to Jenny.

'Miss Duff, do you remember . . . ?'

'What? Remember what, Beattie?'

But the older woman had dried up again.

'Och, it was nothing very important. I forget what I was going to say.'

Nevertheless, there was something on the older woman's mind, decided Jenny. It was something Beattie would no doubt discuss with her in her own good time.

★ ★ ★

Jenny looked very smart on Sunday when she walked over to the schoolhouse. She wore her new suit in the lovely rich brown colour, and her shoes shone with polish. Her new short hairstyle was beginning to settle into neat lines round her head, and Beattie declared that it really suited her very well.

'It looked wispy before, but it's nice now it's grown a wee bit.'

'It's not quite so dry now,' Jenny explained. 'I'm afraid I'd neglected my hair for a long time.'

She had neglected a lot of things about herself, and now there was quite a lot of interest in finding new things she liked to do. It seemed many years since she had gone visiting on a Sunday, for instance, and now she looked forward to her evening with keen enjoyment.

Jean Paterson met her at the door of the pretty cottage built near the school, and escorted her up to the small bright bedroom with attic windows and a sloping roof.

'You can leave your jacket here,' she suggested. 'Jim's already arrived, and I've got the supper all ready. If . . . if you don't mind my saying so, you look very nice, Miss Duff.'

'Thank you, and please call me Jenny,' the younger girl said, rather shyly.

'Jenny, then. Lethansea is doing you a lot of good. I hope you are feeling happier after so many months of trouble in Glasgow.'

She coloured a little.

'I'm sorry . . . maybe you're surprised

that I know your business rather too well. But Dr. Neil Murdoch is a friend of Adam's, and his brother John was very concerned about you.'

'I know,' said Jenny. 'It makes me feel very humble that people should be concerned for me. I don't think of it as nosiness at all. It makes me feel I'm among friends.'

'That's a nice way to feel,' Jean smiled. 'Come on down and I'll introduce you to Jim.'

Jim Paterson was a charming young man, thought Jenny, after an hour or two's acquaintance. He wasn't quite so good-looking at close quarters, but she liked the nice honesty of his face, his quiet good humour and obvious contentment in the company of his brother and sister-in-law.

'I saw you being shown over our works,' he said to Jenny. 'Did you find it interesting?'

'Very,' she said promptly. 'Mr. Maxwell made it all fairly easy for me to understand. I found it exciting when I saw the end product, that it had originally been gathered in from the sea. The sea tangle had all been straightened out, as it were.'

Her eyes were dancing and Jim laughed with her, then his face sobered a little.

'I wish all our tangles could be sorted out so satisfactorily.'

There was a short silence, and Jenny saw the sudden shadow on their faces. Was there some sort of family trouble? she wondered, suddenly uneasy. She had grown to like these people, and hated to think of them being worried in any way.

A moment later Jean was smiling.

'Come on, all of you,' she said gaily. 'I've made a small supper for us all, so let's go into the dining-room. It's only chicken casserole, I'm afraid. I'm not the world's best cook . . . but I hope you'll enjoy it, Jenny.'

'Don't let her fool you,' Jim laughed. 'She's a wonderful cook . . . one of the reasons why I'm always underfoot!

She's just trying to be modest.'

'Not one of my virtues, I'm afraid,' protested Jean. 'I've even been asked to sing at the Christmas concert.'

'Oh dear,' teased Adam. 'Does Mrs. Maxwell want to ruin the concert straight away? In any case, the only one who could play decently was Beryl . . . '

He broke off, and again there was the short, uncomfortable silence. Could it be something to do with Beryl McLean? wondered Jenny, glancing at Jim's face. He was looking down at his plate, his pleasant face rather strained, though he smiled briefly as Jean began to serve the food.

Jenny's thoughts went to Robin, then back again to Jim. No wonder Beryl McLean couldn't make up her mind between these two young men. Both of them had so much to offer, and surely she must have fallen in love with one of them. She must be a very attractive girl to have both young men competing for her.

They even had respect and liking for one another, and no doubt were firm friends. Jenny could imagine that the loser would give in gracefully.

But what if Beryl decided to choose someone else . . . perhaps even in Canada? Could it be that she had written to tell Jim that she was having a happy time there with new friends? Was that why he was looking rather down in the mouth?

Jenny turned again to Jean.

'Beattie tells me Mrs. Maxwell will be after me to see if I'll play for the concert,' she said, her cheeks flushing. 'I'm afraid she's in for a disappointment. I don't play all that well.'

'Oh, you wouldn't have to be an expert,' said Jean quickly. 'I do wish you would. Couldn't we try over one or two of my songs after tea, and see how we get on together?'

'That's a wonderful idea,' said Adam. 'Let Jim and me suffer after eating all this good food.'

'Don't listen to them, Jenny. I'm not *that* bad, or Mrs. Maxwell wouldn't have me. She's got the good of the concert at heart.'

'Then she'd better not ask me,' laughed Jenny.

'We'll see . . . after tea . . . ' decided Jean, looking at her thoughtfully. 'It would be wonderful if you could do it, and keep Carol McLean from getting things all her own way. She's a very overbearing young woman at times. How Beryl has stood her . . . ' She broke off, biting her lip. 'No wonder she hared off, even if she hasn't remembered old friends. Not even Jim.'

The rich colour had crept into Jim's cheeks.

'There was no reason why she should remember me particularly. I'd have thought she'd at least send a postcard to you and Adam. She's worked so closely with you . . . '

'But I thought you had heard from her,' put in Jenny, then drew back.

She should stay out of this discussion, she reminded herself. She didn't even know Beryl McLean and it was none of her business how the other girl chose to behave.

'That was probably Robin,' said Jim, with the first hint of bitterness in his voice, 'though she did promise to write. I can't imagine her not keeping her promise either,' he added, almost arguing with himself. 'She seemed so happy to be going, yet regretful of leaving us.'

'She was sad to go,' said Jean. 'I saw her going and she didn't look herself at all. In fact, she looked tired to death and ready for a good rest.'

'Maybe . . . maybe she's ill,' said Jim, and Jenny could sense his anxiety.

'Maybe,' agreed Adam, 'but didn't Neil McLean say she was fine? Anyway, if it had been illness, you'd think Nancy would have written home. And why should Neil say she was fine, if she really wasn't well? If he'd explained that to us, it would save us worrying, and we could have sent her messages of sympathy . . . '

'That might be it,' said Jean suddenly. 'I bet she's off colour after the long journey, only if she'd let us know, we'd all be sending our sympathy and feeling for her having her holiday spoilt. She wouldn't want that . . . not Beryl . . . '

'No, she wouldn't,' agreed Jim. 'There's no one less selfish than Beryl. I wish we knew for sure though.'

'Can't you ask her brother?' asked Jenny, and the other three were silent.

'He's a queer sort of man,' explained Adam carefully. 'He would think we were prying into his personal affairs, and maybe we would be. Not everyone welcomes the interest of other people in their lives. Neil McLean is one of those sort. He'd immediately get on his high horse and tell us that what his sister does is her business. And he'd be right!'

'But when it's all out of character,' cried Jim. 'You know Beryl. She was . . . is our friend. Even if she . . . she didn't want anything more, she'd never leave us wondering about her unless it's for a very definite reason. I bet she's told Neil to pass on some sort of message and he hasn't done it.'

There was a long silence then Jenny voiced the question which was uppermost in her mind.

'Are you sure she's in Canada?'

Three pairs of eyes turned to her incredulously.

'Where else would she be?' asked Adam. 'If she'd decided against going for some reason or other, she'd just come back home again, surely. Where else could she go?'

Jenny shook her head.

'I . . . I was only wondering. I . . . I don't know her, you see.'

'Yes, we forget about that,' said Jean. 'We expect everybody to know Beryl.'

'I was wondering if I ought to go and see Mr. and Mrs. McLean some time,' admitted Jenny. 'I'm not really getting through to Steven yet. He's a very sensitive little boy.'

'He hasn't had proper security,' growled Adam. 'Neil and Carol don't seem to hit it off too well. That's common knowledge, I'm afraid. Steven's only anchor was Beryl.'

'But that's all wrong,' cried Jenny. 'It should be his parents who can do the most for Steven . . . and I mean by that, give him the most love and the biggest sense of security. Maybe Beryl realised that when she left them, and feels this is a fine chance for the little boy to stand on his own feet, and not lean on her too much. It isn't good for Steven, and it probably isn't good for Beryl either. It will throw responsibility on to her, when she should just be thinking of her own future.'

'Yes,' said Jim, staring at her thoughtfully. 'You've got a point there.'

'So if Steven doesn't thaw out soon, I shall visit Westerhouse and ask for the co-operation of his parents . . . with your permission of course, Mr. Paterson.'

'You have it,' Adam assured her,

'and all the luck you need to go with it.'

'Come on, then,' said Jean, rising from the table. 'Just leave all the washing up for now. I want to try over those songs with Jenny.'

The anxious atmosphere in the little house lightened a little.

'She's determined to sing,' groaned Adam, holding his ears, while his wife poked him playfully as she went to open the lid of the piano, and began to sort out some music.

'Don't either of you two play?' asked Jenny hopefully, turning to the men.

'I play the bagpipes,' Jim told her, 'though Jean doesn't care for them as an accompaniment to her singing.'

Jenny laughed and went to sit down at the piano. She could hardly blame Jean for that!

★ ★ ★

Later, as Jim walked home with her to Howlett Cottage, Jenny remembered

97

the evening with pleasure. Jean's singing had been particularly lovely as she had a fine rich contralto voice, and had chosen some old ballads which suited her voice, and were always popular at concerts.

Jenny had often played for various events at her school in Glasgow. She had allowed her music to slide while her mother was ill, and had imagined that little of her skill would be left through lack of practice, but the accompaniments she played for Jean proved her wrong.

At first her fingers had been a little bit stiff, but gradually she had warmed to her task, her ears listening more to Jean's lovely singing than to her own mistakes.

'Bravo!' applauded Adam when they had finished the third piece. 'That couldn't be better. You won't have any fears over playing for the concert, Jenny. You're every bit as good as Beryl.'

Jenny coloured with pleasure.

'Thank you, but it was Jean's singing which was so beautiful.'

'Which would have sounded terrible if you hadn't been able to play for me properly,' put in Jean handsomely. 'I must say I'm delighted that the concert will go forward as planned. I'll have a word with Mrs. Maxwell so that she doesn't cancel any arrangements.'

'But she hasn't asked me yet,' protested Jenny, 'and I'm . . . I'm not sure about it yet.'

Jim came to smile down at her.

'I think you might as well make up your mind to it, Jenny. You're in Lethansea now, and you'll get no peace till they all get their own way.'

'That's not true, Jim,' protested Jean. 'We're not that bad, surely. Only the concert is for a good cause, and quite a number of old people enjoy it so much. A dance isn't the same for them.'

'Why can't you have both?' asked Jenny. 'The concert, then the dance afterwards. Those people who want to dance could stay behind.'

'But we usually set out the long tables for a meal,' Jean told her doubtfully. 'It would be a job to clear away and prepare the floor for dancing in a short time. We haven't enough help for that.'

'Then hold the dance on another evening . . . say the following week?'

'There's already going to be a Hogmanay Dance,' Jean explained, 'and I think that's enough in a wee place like this.'

'Of course,' said Jenny. 'I didn't know about the Hogmanay Dance.'

'You'll have to go to that,' said Jim. 'Everyone does. It's a real good night, and I'll claim some dances now if I may.'

Jenny's face glowed so that she suddenly looked very attractive, and Jim's smile deepened. 'No doubt I'll have competition,' he added.

'I'd enjoy going to the dance,' she assured him, then turned back to the piano. 'Shall we have one or two more songs round the piano, then I really must get back.'

Walking home with Jim, Jenny felt more alive than she had done for years. The sky was clear and bright, and the sound of the sea was like another kind of music. She had enjoyed meeting Jim Paterson, though in many ways it had been a disturbing evening. The shadow of Beryl McLean had seemed to fall over them, and hadn't really gone away, even now.

'It would be nice to see you again, Jenny,' Jim was saying as he shook hands outside the gate. 'Wouldn't you like a day out in Girvan next Saturday? Do you know Girvan well, or would I have the pleasure of taking you round?'

'You'd have the pleasure of taking me round,' admitted Jenny. 'I only went there once, on a trip from Sunday School when I was about nine. I have very happy memories of that day.'

'Next Saturday, then,' said Jim.

'Oh no!' she cried, remembering. 'I've promised to go out with Robin Maxwell next Saturday. He's taking me sightseeing, too.'

'Oh well . . . ' Jim gave a rueful laugh. 'Some other time, then, Jenny. Goodnight.'

'Goodnight,' she echoed, and let herself into the cottage.

It was rather interesting, she thought that night, as she lay in bed, that when she turned down Robin's date because she was already going to the Paterson's, he had immediately made another. But when she turned Jim down, he had only said he would see her soon again.

It was obvious, too, that neither of them was secretly engaged to Beryl.

'But at least she won't need to worry about me,' thought Jenny, plumping up her pillow. 'I'm no rival for her.'

Perhaps the two men were well aware of that, she thought wryly. Perhaps that was why they were both seeking her company.

Some of Jenny's new feeling of well-being evaporated a little, but she was too tired to care very much. Her bed was warm and comfortable, and she was soon fast asleep.

5

The autumn term had gone very quickly, Jenny thought, as plans for Christmas began to loom up. She decided on her own favourite version of the usual nativity play for her children, one in which every child would take part. There would be enough angel parts to suit all the girls, and the boys could be shepherds, with Steven McLean as the Archangel Gabriel. He looked the part, she decided, with his lovely little solemn face, large dark eyes and curly hair.

But Steven hung back when Jenny tried to interest the children in her play.

'Don't you want to be the Archangel Gabriel?' she asked, taking the small boy's hand.

'Please, miss, he's always a Three Wise Man,' one of the other children explained.

Jenny hid a smile.

'Would you rather be one of the Three Wise Men?' she asked Steven gently, and he nodded, if reluctantly.

Unfortunately she had already chosen her Three Wise Men, and a look at the small stubborn faces informed her they were pleased with the arrangement, and didn't want an exchange of parts.

'Oh dear,' said Jenny to herself. 'I haven't managed this very well, have I?'

'Look, Steven,' she said, 'couldn't you be different this year? Wouldn't you like to have a change and not be the same as last year?'

The small boy's face began to crumple, then the features became wooden again, almost by an effort of will.

'All right,' he agreed, but Jenny didn't feel she had won a victory. She sent the class back to their places, and prepared to read them a story, but her mind was still very much on Steven. It was disturbing to see a child of his age so quiet and acquiescent.

She thought of the fine white house called Westerhouse, but although it was beautiful, it repelled her, and she had put off the task which she knew would be hers one day. Apart from one afternoon when she first came to the school, and Adam had arranged for the parents to meet and welcome her, she hadn't really got to know many of the parents. If the McLeans had been at that meeting, she couldn't bring them to mind.

Now she felt she wanted to talk to Carol McLean. Perhaps it wouldn't help, and Steven would continue to be the same quiet little boy, but at least she would have tried.

It was early evening when Jenny made her way along the shore path to Westerhouse. This time she walked determinedly through the gateway, where the lovely wrought-iron gates had been hooked back, no doubt to allow access with a car, and straight up to the front door, her feet crunching on the gravel.

A young girl, no doubt a home help or au pair girl, asked her to wait in the hall, then came back to show her into a large drawing-room, saying that Mrs. McLean would see her presently, when she was free. At the moment she was speaking on the telephone.

Jenny looked round the beautiful room which had been furnished without counting the cost. Carol McLean must have excellent taste, she thought, admiring the lovely green carpeting which toned so well with the long velvet curtains. The settees and easy chairs were large and sumptuous, but Jenny found herself sitting up rather uncomfortably, as thought afraid to make a mark on the cushions.

It was a room to admire, she decided, much more than a room in which to relax. She could see evidence of Neil McLean in the pipe rack and several magazines not usually of interest to women, but again he seemed to have left little imprint on the room. Neither was there a toy in sight.

It was some time before Carol McLean came to find her, then she walked gracefully into the room, her flimsy dress clinging delicately to her body. Jenny blinked and could see at once where Steven got his angelic looks. He was so very like his mother.

'You're . . . Miss . . . ?'

Mrs. McLean was holding out a pretty white hand.

'Duff.'

'Miss Duff. You're from the organising committee, I suppose? It's about the dance . . . ?'

'No, I'm Miss Duff, Steven's teacher,' said Jenny firmly. 'I'm taking Miss McLean's place now that she's gone to Canada.'

'I see.'

The bright smile froze a little and the dark eyes grew appraising.

'I'm sorry, I should have recognised you, perhaps . . . ' She shrugged as though to indicate that Jenny wasn't the sort of person to stick in one's mind. 'What can I do for you, Miss Duff?'

Jenny was unsure where to begin. She could feel the lack of sympathy in this woman, and knew how difficult it was going to be to try to explain her disquiet over the child. Yet, thinking about Steven, her resolution hardened and her chin firmed.

'I came to talk to you about Steven,' she began.

Carol McLean drifted over to a small table and selected a cigarette from a silver box, picking up a table lighter. Jenny was prepared to refuse the offer of one, but there was no need. It wasn't offered.

'I hope this won't take a long time, Miss Duff,' the older girl said crisply. 'I have an appointment for this evening and I haven't got very long to spare. I would have thought that any problems over Steven could be sorted out quite satisfactorily between you and Mr. Paterson. He's hardly old enough for us to worry if he's slow in some things. Surely he's got plenty of time for that?'

'Of course, but . . .'

'Besides, I would like him to go to another school of my own choice in another two years. I must make it plain, Miss Duff, that Steven is only in your class because my husband and sister-in-law feel he is better to be at the local school while he is still so young. I've agreed to this, but only until he is a little older.'

'Nevertheless, while he is in my care, I'm sure you'll wish me to do my best for him,' said Jenny as smoothly as she could manage.

The interview was going to be even more difficult than she had supposed, and she bit her lip, wondering which was the best way to tackle Mrs. McLean. Finally she decided that it would be best to be completely straightforward.

'Your son, I feel, is unhappy, Mrs. McLean,' she said, quietly. 'He is worrying about something and I can't bring out the best in him unless we find out what it is.'

Carol stared at her.

'But if you're making him unhappy, Miss Duff, surely it's your duty to correct that. Aren't you trained to make lessons interesting to children these days so that they won't be worried by the three Rs, or whatever it is . . . '

'I think his problems come from outside school,' said Jenny bravely, and there was an icy silence.

'You are suggesting I make my child unhappy at home?' asked Carol softly.

'No, not quite . . . '

Jenny tried to hold on to some clear thinking.

'I want him to do something different for the Christmas play,' she began, deciding that some sort of explanation might be best. 'He was one of the Three Wise Men last year, no doubt because he's tall for his age. This year I'd like him to be the Archangel Gabriel.'

Carol laughed. 'And Steven kicked,' she said gently. 'Good for him!'

'No. No, it wasn't like that,' said Jenny. 'He didn't really protest. In fact, he . . . he said he'd do it.'

'Then why come to me? What an extraordinary thing! I could understand a teacher having it out with the parents of a disobedient boy, but not an obedient one! That's rather too much, Miss Duff.'

'Please try to understand,' said Jenny doggedly. 'Don't you see? He accepts things like this too easily . . . too woodenly! He doesn't show his feelings enough.'

'You'd prefer him to have tantrums?'

Jenny paused, aware that a well-built dark-haired man had come into the house and was walking towards them in the sitting-room. She stood up, feeling defeated.

'Obviously I can't make you appreciate my concern,' she said evenly. 'I . . . I think I'd better go.'

'I'm sorry,' Carol Mclean told her. 'When you've got a more serious complaint, I'll be glad to listen. Oh,

Neil dear, this is Miss Duff, Steven's teacher. She thinks he's too obedient!'

Neil McLean acknowledged Jenny with an inclination of the head, and without any real show of interest.

'She wants him to be an angel in the nativity play.'

'Oh, good . . . good . . . ' Neil McLean walked vaguely round the room. 'Good of you to come and tell us, Miss Duff.'

'Your teaching methods must be unusual,' Carol said, 'or the children you've been used to. Where did you teach before coming to Lethansea?'

'Glasgow.'

'Glasgow?' For a moment Neil McLean turned to her sharply, then he bent to pick up his pipe.

'You'll have to get used to Steven,' said Carol gently. 'I don't think you'll find him very different from any other well-brought-up child of his age.'

Jenny nodded, biting back an angry retort. She had taught very fine children as well as badly trained ones, but it was pointless discussing this with Carol McLean. As her feet crunched again on the gravel, she looked round for signs that a small boy lived here. There was no toy bicycle or pedal car, and no discarded ball or toy truck.

As she walked along, Jenny could feel the angry colour glowing in her cheeks, and her heart grew heavy as she thought about the small, very quiet boy with the lovely dark unhappy eyes. The child did need help . . . she was sure of it!

Was he missing his Aunt Beryl, or was something else worrying the child?

Jenny shivered when she thought of the house she had just left. It was a beautiful house, but how much more beautiful it would have seemed if she could have heard the happy laughter of a little boy.

* * *

'You're very thoughtful this evening.'

Jenny started guiltily as she walked slowly along by the sea, her thoughts still with Steven McLean, then she smiled as Robin Maxwell fell into step beside her.

It was a pleasant evening, but the air had grown chilly, reminding Jenny that winter would soon be here. She spoke these thoughts aloud to Robin.

'I was just thinking that we're almost into winter now.'

'Well, there's a lot to be said for the winter months, don't you think?'

'Christmas, you mean?'

'Christmas, of course. But it always seems to me a time of rest, of preparations for spring and the full enjoyment of summer. Winter's a time when we're glad to sit round the fire, or if we feel like a challenge, we can take a fine bracing walk out in the cold clear air.'

'Is that what it's like in Lethansea? I can only think of cold wet streets and influenza.'

'Shame on you!' he teased. 'Where's that fine spirit of yours? And surely it wasn't just thoughts of winter which brought the worried look to your eyes?'

The smile left Jenny's lips.

'I . . . I was worried about one of my children,' she told him honestly.

'Oh dear. Nothing wrong, I hope. I know most of the parents of your children, you see. Many of the men are employed at the Works.'

'I know.'

Jenny nodded rather uncomfortably. She didn't find it easy to talk about the McLeans to Robin in view of his friendship with Beryl.

Had Robin now heard from Beryl? she wondered. If only she herself could write to Beryl McLean and ask for guidance over Steven. Yet that wouldn't do, she decided, dismissing the thought almost immediately. The other girl was on a well-deserved holiday, and from what she had heard of her, Beryl would worry a great deal if she thought Steven wasn't happy. It would spoil her holiday and Jenny could never do that.

Yet how could she get through to the little boy and find out what he was bottling up? Jenny had seen this happen before with other children and felt she must do all in her power to reassure Steven.

'Do you know the McLeans well, Robin?' Jenny asked at length.

He was silent for a long moment.

'As well as anybody knows them, I suppose.'

'It's Steven I'm worried about. I . . . I don't think that child's too happy. Perhaps he's missing her aunt, but I just can't get through to him. He's too obedient, if you know what I mean.'

Robin didn't laugh. He knew exactly what Jenny meant.

'I went to see his parents this evening, but I had difficulty in explaining this to them. In fact, I made a rotten job of it, and maybe I've just made things worse. I wish I could make them understand.'

Robin's mouth grew rather hard.

'There was always a big difference between Beryl and Neil,' he said bluntly. 'Neil never lets you see what he's thinking. I often used to wish Beryl would go away from those two, and that's the truth.'

Jenny believed him, and thought she could read unhappiness in his voice. She stole a glance at the man walking by her side and sighed a little. Love didn't follow any rules, and didn't always allow one to be sensible. No doubt Robin still cared for Beryl, so it was no use hoping . . .

Jenny's hand almost flew to her mouth as she realised where her thoughts were taking her. She really had been hoping that Robin didn't want Beryl McLean, and might want someone else one day . . . might even want Jenny?

Her heart raced and her cheeks grew warm at the thought. Had Robin Maxwell really come to mean all that to her? Jenny felt confused, but knew almost certainly that even though she had only known him a few short weeks, he had become important to her.

He took her arm as they walked over some rough ground and she jerked at his touch.

'Steady,' he said, misunderstanding. 'You'll have to get used to walking along the sea shore. It isn't exactly a city pavement.'

'I like it much better,' she assured him, rather breathlessly. 'I've come to love the sea.'

They paused to watch the waves rippling against the shore, dark grey in the gathering dusk.

'If you can't make progress with young Steven, tell me again and I'll see what I can do. I doubt, though, whether I'll have any great influence with the McLeans.'

He said this rather dryly, but Jenny thanked him, feeling that it helped even to talk it over with Robin.

'Don't forget our date on Saturday,' he reminded her, when they parted beside the cottage. 'Oh, and my mother wants you to have tea with us in the evening. I rather think she's got designs on you for the Christmas concert.'

'I know,' said Jenny ruefully. 'Beattie's mentioned it already.'

'You shouldn't be so talented, Jenny,' Robin told her, laughing. 'You'll never get away with it in Lethansea. Every talent gets used to the utmost here. We have to go in for quality, if we don't have quantity.'

'I'd hardly call my small talent quality,' countered Jenny, and for answer Robin grabbed her in a bear-like hug.

'No modesty,' he informed her, and gave her a quick kiss.

Jenny went home with burning cheeks and wildly beating heart, which soon changed to depression. It hadn't been the sort of kiss she'd wanted from Robin. If he couldn't fall in love with her, she didn't want him to kiss her at all.

But Jenny found herself looking forward to her date with Robin on Saturday with eager anticipation. She had taken herself to task, and decided that her relationship with Robin must be a sensible one. He was never likely to fall in love with her, so she must be happy with his friendship.

Beattie took a keen interest in her date, and decided that Miss Duff looked just fine in the pretty white dress she had chosen. It was trimmed with pale green and she had green accessories.

'You're very smart, Miss Duff,' she commented, helping Jenny into her warm coat. 'You're no' like the lass who came here in August. Lethansea has made a difference to you.'

Jenny agreed, thinking that it had made more of a difference even than Beattie imagined.

Robin had cleaned and polished the car, and it looked very smart indeed.

'I thought we'd maybe go down to Girvan, then along to Newton Stewart via The Knowe. Would you like that, Jenny?'

'I'm with you today,' she smiled. 'You know the district and I don't, so I'm happy to go where you suggest.'

'Come on then, let's go.'

It was a wonderful day and Jenny thoroughly enjoyed exploring all the small towns and villages which Robin knew so well, and had always taken for granted.

Now he looked at the pretty countryside, and charming houses, through Jenny's eyes and enjoyed the trip every bit as much as she did. She loved the gentle hills and small, often unexpected, lochs, the bubbling rivers and rolling green fields. They stopped for lunch at a small country hotel, and Jenny relaxed happily, and smiled at Robin, blushing to find him eyeing her intently.

'Have you got plans made for when your time in Lethansea is finished?' he asked, after a long moment.

'I shall have to go back to Glasgow, back to my home there.'

'You still have your home, then?'

'Of course. I only let it, you see. I . . . I felt I couldn't leave myself without a home, though it's lonely now that I'm on my own.'

'Tell me about it,' he invited, as the waitress served their lunch.

'Nothing much to tell. I was happy there . . . when we were all a family.'

She began to describe her life when she was younger and both her parents alive, remembering again the happy times and all the fun and laughter.

Robin listened intently, his eyes on her small expressive face, thinking how attractive she looked. Jenny never saw the varied expressions on her own face, and how vividly alive it could be. She only saw her features in repose, and couldn't know that she often looked very different when she was describing things which interested her.

'What about your friend . . . Charles,

is it? Is he part of that life, Jenny?'

Robin's voice was very casual, but she didn't notice. She wondered if he was concerned for the fact that she was now very much alone.

'We've been friends ever since I went to teach in Grammar School,' she said frankly. 'I'm not really alone, you know.'

'Of course not. I only wondered ... will I be congratulating him one of these days?'

The warm colour flooded her cheeks.

'I . . . I hardly think so.'

'He's a fool if he doesn't want to make your friendship more permanent,' said Robin, a trifle roughly.

'Oh, he does!' Jenny assured him. 'Charles isn't a fool . . . I mean . . .'

She broke off, confused, and a trifle cross. Robin had no right to ask her questions. It wasn't as though he cared for her and felt that her welfare was his business. He was interested in people, but in her case, he was taking his interest a little too far.

'Charles and I understand each other,' she said quietly.

'Oh, I see,' said Robin. 'I'm glad for you, Jenny. Would you like more coffee?'

'No, thank you.'

She collected her bag and went to have a wash. The sparkle had gone out of her eyes, and her own plain little face gazed back at her from a long, very bright mirror. It reminded Jenny that she must keep things in perspective, and she was herself again when she returned to the car.

'Home, then,' he suggested. 'Mother is very keen that we spare some time for her.'

Robin grinned. He was very fond of his busy mother whom he called a 'committee woman.' Mrs. Maxwell took this in good part, and didn't bother to deny it.

'Somebody has to take the lead,' she often explained. 'If we all sit back, then there will be no one to step forward.'

Robin was thinking of that as he

drove Jenny home. Perhaps he was inclined to do too much sitting back. Perhaps some time he ought to take a leaf out of his mother's book!

* * *

Mrs. Maxwell was a tall, well-built lady and her greying hair still had a touch of fiery red lights showing from where Robin got his colouring. She was a bustling, efficient woman whom Jenny had found rather formidable at first, but she was now aware of the kind heart underneath all the efficiency and was at ease with the older woman.

'It's a blessing you can play the piano,' Mrs. Maxwell told her, after they all sat down to tea. 'I had lessons myself once, but no gift at all. Nor has Robin. We even tried him at the violin, but no one could stand the noise he made.'

Robin was grinning broadly. 'I can sing, though,' he assured Jenny.

'Unfortunately not in tune,' his

mother informed her. 'He's got a big voice, but no idea how to use it. No, I'm afraid I have to find my musical inspiration outside the home, Jenny, and maybe that's why I enjoy organising the concert. We've got a lot of talent in Lethansea and the surrounding district, and folk enjoy putting on a show. It brings the people in from other villages and we can all have a good night together. Better than noisy dance music.'

'I wondered why you didn't have both,' put in Jenny, 'but Mrs. Paterson says you have a Hogmanay Dance.'

'That's right,' said Mrs. Maxwell. 'That's what I told Carol McLean. Get your dancing done then, is what I told her, and we'll keep Christmas for our concert. What's more, we should make it a concert every year. She only suggested a dance to put me out, anyway. Don't think I can't see through her, and don't think I'll let her get away with it either.'

To Jenny's surprise Mrs. Maxwell's

voice suddenly softened.

'There I go again, when I should know better, letting my tongue 'clip cloots', as they say. Maybe the poor lass hasn't got her sorrows to seek. At any rate, I'm glad you're going to help, my dear.'

Jenny nodded. She had given up telling people she was no expert. She knew she would just have to do her best.

'I'm looking forward to the meeting on Wednesday night,' said Mrs. Maxwell with satisfaction, and obviously forgetting, again, to be charitable. 'Carol McLean thinks she's got us down an alley. She doesn't know you can play, dear. At one time she and Neil never bothered about village affairs because they were always off to the bright lights. But now rumour has it that money doesn't flow so freely these days, so she's turning her attention to the village. No doubt she feels she should be running the place, but I've been organising things for years and making a good job of it, so I'm not going to let her spoil things. Mrs. Dewar, the minister's wife, used to do it with me, but we lost her a year ago. I miss Emma Dewar a lot, and I know she wouldn't have Carol at the head of things. She isn't capable in the right way . . .'

Jenny listened while Mrs. Maxwell rambled on, and now she looked at Robin's mother with sympathy. There was a hint of loneliness in the brisk voice, and she guessed that Mrs. Maxwell needed her organising as an outlet for her energies.

Her thoughts turned to Carol McLean, and she wondered a little if she'd judged her a little too quickly. Was Carol, too, perhaps a bit unhappy when she wanted to interfere in the affairs of the village, and make changes which would bring more prominence to herself? Perhaps some sort of inner unhappiness would account for her inability to see that her small son needed more attention than he was getting.

Jenny came out of her thoughts to find Robin eyeing her, a trifle anxiously.

'You don't mind playing, do you, Jenny?' he asked. 'Don't let Mother bulldoze you into it if you'd rather not.'

'Bulldoze?' echoed Mrs. Maxwell. 'What a thing for my own son to say!'

There had been a note of banter in their voices and Jenny wasn't deceived. She knew there was a very happy and understanding relationship between Robin and his mother. They loved each other, and allowed each other to live their own lives.

'It's all right, Robin,' she said gently. 'I'm not being bulldozed, as you put it. It's just that I'm not an expert by any means, but I'm willing to help all I can.'

'That's the spirit,' said Robin's mother approvingly. 'The meeting is at seven-thirty in the small church hall. You'll manage that, won't you?'

'Oh, but surely you won't want me . . . I mean, I'm not a member of your committee.'

'Co-opted on,' said Mrs. Maxwell firmly. 'We'll have a lot to decide, and you'd better be there. We want something different this time from the last concert, which was to give Beryl a parting gift . . . '

She stopped and glanced briefly at Robin. Jenny was aware of a small uncomfortable silence, and wondered how Mrs. Maxwell had felt about Beryl. Perhaps she was looking forward to having a daughter-in-law just like her, who would be a good companion for her, too.

Jenny was aware of a small stab of nostalgia as she looked round the comfortable room. The Maxwells had a lovely home. The Whins was a bigger house than she had imagined from her first acquaintance with it. It was a good solid house, sitting cosily in a rather haphazard garden which showed evidence of being lovingly tended nevertheless.

The house was gabled, with unexpected rooms jutting out at odd corners, and Jenny liked the old rich mahogany furniture and the delicate china ornaments. Mrs. Maxwell's biggest extravagance seemed to be rich carpeting and the only place which had escaped was the kitchen, as Jenny found when she helped to clear the table.

She had interrupted the awkward silence by offering to do the washing up, and was pleased when Mrs. Maxwell leapt at it.

'We'll do it together, Jenny,' she said. 'Robin, put more logs on the fire in the sitting-room. It's getting chilly now in the evenings.'

The washing up was soon done, though this time it was Jenny who had to do the talking, as the older woman asked about her life in Glasgow, and sympathised with her over the loss of her parents.

'It's sad for a young girl like you to be on her own,' she said gently. 'You must come and talk to me whenever you like.'

'Thank you,' Jenny told her, a trifle huskily.

But she knew she wouldn't come in very often. There was a queer ache of longing in her heart to be part of this small family, and as she sat in the sitting-room while Mrs. Maxwell clicked happily at her knitting, and Robin reached over to fill his pipe, Jenny almost felt she was already part of it all.

'I must go,' she said, after a short while. 'Beattie will be wondering where I am.'

'She knows you're here,' said Mrs. Maxwell comfortably, but Robin saw Jenny's hesitation and rose immediately.

'I'll walk back home with you,' he said easily.

'Don't forget, Wednesday at seven-thirty,' said Mrs. Maxwell firmly.

'All . . . all right,' agreed Jenny.

She wasn't really looking forward to that meeting. It might mean another clash with Carol McLean and she didn't want to be too much at loggerheads with her because of little Steven.

'Thank you for a lovely evening,' she said shyly, and Robin's mother suddenly bent and gave her a quick kiss.

'You're welcome, Jenny,' she said. 'Don't forget . . . come and see me any time at all.'

For some reason Jenny's throat stung as she walked the short distance home beside Robin.

She could hardly find words to bid him goodnight and beyond a tightening of his hand on her arm, he let her go and stood looking after her thoughtfully. She could smell tobacco in the cool, clear fresh air, and tried to remind herself that she must treat their friendship sensibly.

Yet falling in love wasn't at all sensible, as she reminded herself again. It created complications and difficulties she could well do without.

'Did you have a good day, Miss

Duff?' Beattie was asking as she rose from beside the fire.

'Very good,' smiled Jenny.

But she was rather subdued, and Beattie looked at her closely, then held her tongue.

6

On Monday morning Jenny woke to the sound of rain lashing on the windows and quickly got out of bed, pulling back the curtains. It rained quite often in Lethansea, quick showers which cleared just as quickly and were dried by the winds which followed, but this morning the skies were leaden and the sea looked ominous as it lashed against the rocks.

'A letter for you, Miss Duff,' Beattie told her, when she went downstairs to breakfast. 'From Glasgow again.'

Jenny sometimes felt rather touched that Charles had never stopped writing, especially as he now wrote friendly letters which kept her in touch with her old life, and did not try to intrude into the new.

This morning, however, he reminded her that in a few weeks it would be Christmas.

'Why not come to Glasgow one weekend soon?' he asked. 'The shops are looking their best and Mr. Todd, the janitor's wife, is more than willing to give you a room for a night or two. We could, perhaps, go to a show or something . . . whatever you like . . . '

It used to be whatever Charles liked, thought Jenny, with a wry smile, then felt a little ashamed. He obviously wanted to stay friends with her, and this was his way of showing it.

Jenny looked out at the rain which was making wet puddles in the roadway. Her raincoat wasn't heavy enough to withstand a drenching like this, and besides, she did have Christmas shopping to do. It would be rather nice to go back to Glasgow.

'I think I'll go back home some weekend before Christmas,' she said to Beattie. 'I've got some shopping to do and it would be a good opportunity.'

'You're going back to Glasgow.'

Beattie made the statement rather thoughtfully, and Jenny turned to look

136

at her. Surely it shouldn't matter to Beattie whether she went back home or not.

'You . . . you don't mind, do you, Beattie?' she asked a trifle sharply, and the older woman coloured guiltily.

'Och no, of course not. It'll do you the world of good to get away for a wee while. You'll have extra work, too, with that concert coming up, but I think you'll find it worth while.'

'I'm sure I will,' said Jenny, rather mechanically.

In Glasgow concerts had come and gone enjoyed by pupils and teachers alike, but this one seemed to loom over her a great deal more.

'I'll have to get a move on,' she told Beattie, glancing at the clock. 'It won't do if I'm the one to be late.'

Perhaps the rain had depressed her, but Jenny found herself having more than a little difficulty with her class. For once Steven McLean had chosen to be noisy instead of quiet, and Jenny wondered later, rather wearily, which was worst. His shrill laughter had encouraged the others to misbehave, and she had had to use all her tact and patience to deal with them.

'Oh dear, I must be slipping,' she confided to Adam Paterson, during break. 'They aren't easy to control today.'

'Some days are just like that,' Adam agreed. 'You'll have to be firm with the worst offender.'

'Unfortunately that's Steven again,' Jenny told him ruefully. 'I've been thinking recently that he was beginning to accept me, but pride often goes before a fall.'

'You'll need more patience with him,' agreed Adam. 'How's the nativity play coming on?'

'Not so bad. Most of the children are enjoying it, and entering into the spirit of it all with enthusiasm.'

'And young Steven?'

Jenny bit her lip. 'Maybe I made a mistake trying to make him do a different part. He'd have been happier with the old familiar one from last year, I think.'

'He should be able to accept change,' said Adam.

'Sometimes he goes through it perfectly, and sometimes he holds everything up. I'd get infuriated if I couldn't see that the little boy is as much a trial to himself as to anybody. He's a bundle of nerves.'

Jenny went back to her class and soon began to interest them in a group project to make a decoration for Christmas. She pinned up a long roll of heavy paper on the wall and set the children to cut out fir trees, small houses and Father Christmas with his sledge pulled by reindeer.

'You can make a robin,' she told Steven. 'I'll show you how to do it.'

The small boy stood beside her, breathing heavily, while she showed him how to cut out the little bird and stick on a scarlet breast and a bright beady eye. For once she could feel the child's interest, and she turned to him and put the robin into his hand, he suddenly smiled and it seemed as though the sun had come out.

'Do you like it, Steven?' she asked softly.

'It's a nice robin,' he told her gravely.

'Then you make another one the same and we'll stick them on to the picture.'

Again the smile flashed out and Steven nodded happily.

But on Tuesday she found that the robins had been taken from the picture, and she stared at the empty spaces thoughtfully, then turned to look at Steven sitting quietly in class. Again he had the withdrawn look on his face, and Jenny felt just as defeated as ever.

* * *

She didn't particularly look forward to the committee meeting on Wednesday evening, and to openly opposing Carol McLean. By now the other woman would have heard that she had agreed to play for the concert, and Jenny wondered how she would react to the news. Perhaps Carol would have shrugged it off if she hadn't gone to see her about Steven. Something which was a matter of minor importance might now become rather more serious, because of the personalities involved.

Jenny hated to think of becoming bad friends with anyone, least of all Carol McLean. She knew she was going to have to approach her again, one day, over Steven, and this time she would have to make the other woman understand. She didn't want any other issue to be an irritation.

But the meeting went surprisingly smoothly. Carol turned up looking like an exotic bird among a flock of sparrows, in a bright scarlet coat and long black boots.

'So I propose that the concert goes ahead,' boomed Mrs. Maxwell, after she had introduced Jenny, and thanked her for being able to take over from

Beryl in such an all-round way.

'Please yourself,' agreed Carol. 'We've been bored before, and no doubt we can all be bored again.'

'I think I can speak for others, as well as for myself, when I say we won't be bored in the least,' said Mrs. Maxwell coldly. 'As to a possible dance, there's one already being organised for Hogmanay. Those among us who like dancing can look forward to that.'

'I had been thinking of a real dance, not square dancing all the time,' put in Carol.

'We try to please the majority of people, not individuals,' returned Mrs. Maxwell. 'We realise fashions change, but I think our young people will agree that the organisers try to cater for all tastes. The dance is aimed to please as many people as possible.'

'And ends up pleasing nobody,' said Carol.

'Oh, I'm sure it's very much enjoyed,' put in another member, and a buzz of voices started up.

'We're wandering from the point,' said Mrs. Maxwell, bringing the meeting to order. 'I think we ought to put this to the vote. Concert or dance.'

The voting for the concert was eleven to one, and Carol's eyes met Jenny's, a hint of mischief in them.

Why, she's only doing it out of boredom, she thought, with a sense of shock. She doesn't care at all about a dance. Again she wondered about the lovely fair-haired woman, and the quiet withdrawn man who was her husband and Beryl McLean's brother. She could sense the unhappiness in that house and wondered what had caused it, and what effect it would have on little Steven if it wasn't put right.

Jenny listened rather vaguely while a programme was drawn up for the concert, and smiled when she caught Jean Paterson's eye. Later, when they left the meeting, Jean caught hold of her arm.

'We can walk back together, Jenny,' she said.

143

'I . . . I came with Mrs. Maxwell,' said Jenny, her eyes going to where the older woman was still discussing points with one or two others.

'Oh, she'll be ages,' Jean told her. 'Hang on and I'll have a quick word with her.'

Mrs. Maxwell signalled for Jenny to go on ahead, and Jean again took her arm.

'Well, did you enjoy the meeting?' she asked.

'Not too much,' said Jenny honestly. 'I felt strange, and I didn't want to get on the wrong side of Mrs. McLean.'

Jean laughed and squeezed her arm. 'You'll have to get used to that sort of thing. As a matter of fact, we all really enjoyed it. You'll soon get to know the others, and find them all aching to help.'

Jenny considered. Perhaps what Jean said was right.

'We'll have one or two rehearsals which will sound terrible, then the concert will go like a bomb and you'll wonder why you ever worried about it.'

'I hope you're right,' laughed Jenny.

As they reached the Paterson house, Jean invited Jenny in for a quick cup of tea.

'Oh no, I mustn't,' she protested. 'It's rather late and Beattie will have a hot drink ready. I . . . ' She broke off as Jim Paterson loomed up in the doorway.

'Then I'll walk home with you,' he offered. 'I was just going, anyway. Goodnight, Jean . . . Adam!'

His voice rose and a moment later Adam, too, appeared at the door. There was much talking and laughing, but Jim fell into step beside Jenny as they walked the short distance to Howlett Cottage.

'How did it go?' he asked.

'All right, I think. Jean said everyone enjoyed the meeting, and I think she's probably right. I don't know people well enough yet to feel what they're thinking, if you know what I mean.'

Jim laughed. 'I know what you mean.'

In the semi-darkness he looked very tall and dark and Jenny could see the flash of his teeth when he smiled.

'How about a night off tomorrow night?' he suggested. 'Put it all out of your mind for a while, and let's go into Ayr. Would a film be all right for you?'

Jenny hesitated only for a second. It would be nice to go out for an evening.

'Thank you,' she told him happily, as she paused to talk to him at the gate. They stood aside as the lights of a car lit up the roadway, and a moment later Robin drove past, tooting his horn as he recognised them. He must have picked up Mrs. Maxwell at the hall, thought Jenny, seeing her in the passenger seat.

'Goodnight, Jenny,' said Jim, as she walked in through the gate. 'I'll call round for you about seven.'

'Goodnight,' she answered.

There had been nothing wrong with

the evening, she thought later, but she was conscious of a vague feeling of dissatisfaction which she couldn't quite explain. She had quarrelled with no one, and she had a date for the next evening with a very nice young man. Yet wouldn't it have made her even more happy if the young man had been Robin?

Jenny threw off her thoughts and reminded herself firmly that it was best for her to go out with Jim, too. She must remember that they were only friends, and value that friendship.

Before going to bed, she made out a list of shopping which could be done when she went to Glasgow, and added a new dress for the concert. She had an idea where she could get one which would be very special, deciding that she wanted to look nice on this occasion.

★ ★ ★

Jenny found herself looking forward to her date with Jim, and she was ready, waiting for him, when he drove up in rather an old car.

Beattie had been interested in all her outings, and had remarked jokingly that Miss Duff was certainly stepping into Miss Beryl's shoes, then blushed a little, feeling she had put her foot in it. 'I'm sorry, Miss Duff,' she apologised. 'That wasn't a very nice remark to make. Take no notice of what I say.'

Jenny's eyes crinkled with laughter, though the remark put things into perspective for her.

'I'm a good stand-in,' she remarked lightly, 'ready to step down when the star appears.'

Beattie's eyes grew serious.

'Don't say that, Miss Duff,' she said sharply. 'You're a good enough star yourself. You're quite different from Miss Beryl, but you've got your own place here among us. We realise we haven't got you for long, but you're making your niche here just the same.'

Jenny felt a sudden lump rising in her throat.

'Thank you, Beattie,' she said huskily, and on impulse kissed the older woman's cheek, as Jim drove up to the door. 'I don't expect I'll be late.'

Jenny thoroughly enjoyed her night out with Jim Paterson, finding him an entertaining companion. It was some time since she'd seen a film, and the one Jim had chosen was bright and amusing. Jenny felt very indulged, especially when Jim produced a lovely box of chocolates and laid them on her lap.

'Oh, what luxury!' she said laughingly.

Jim found her appreciation rather touching. It was relaxing to take Jenny out, he mused, since she was so frankly enjoying herself.

'I thought you'd have lived a very social life in Glasgow,' he said, a question in his voice.

'No, not very. I went out quite a lot with Charles, but mainly to school events like plays and concerts given by the children.'

'Charles?'

'I forgot you didn't meet Charles Cairns when he came to Lethansea a few weeks ago. Robin Maxwell met him, though, and gave us a lift to the station.'

'Oh,' said Jim thoughtfully. 'Is Charles a special friend, then?'

'We're not engaged, if that's what you mean,' she told him frankly, then hesitated, wondering if she could be equally curious about Jim's affairs.

'What about you?' she asked at length. 'I . . . I heard you and Miss McLean were rather special friends.'

Jim became rather withdrawn.

'I thought so, too,' he said quietly, 'but I know now I was wrong. Beryl must live her own life, and . . . ' he paused, then continued firmly, ' . . . and I must learn to live mine. One can't push other people's lives around to suit oneself. We've all got to be happy in our own way, and allow each other to be happy, too.'

'Not make demands on each other,' said Jenny.

'Exactly,' said Jim firmly.

They were making their way to where Jim had parked his car, and Jenny climbed in silently, her thoughts busy. She didn't know whether or not she agreed with Jim. If he really loved Beryl, as she suspected he did, then perhaps he hadn't tried hard enough to win her. Was he the sort of man whose pride was stronger than his love?

'You're very quiet,' he said gently, as they drove home.

'I was thinking,' she admitted, blushing, aware that she couldn't share her thoughts with him. Jim's affairs were nothing to do with her.

'I've enjoyed this evening,' she said, changing the subject.

'Then let's do it again some time.'

'Yes, let's,' she laughed.

Suddenly Jim stopped the car and drew her close to him, and was kissing her before she had time to push him away.

'No, Jim,' she protested. 'I . . . I'm sorry.'

Immediately he was contrite.

'I'm sorry, too, Jenny. I ... I suppose I was a bit lonely. Is it ... Charles?'

She shook her head.

'No, not Charles. Not anybody, really.' She drew a deep breath. 'But I don't really like being a substitute for someone else, Jim.'

'What do you mean?' he asked.

'I think you love Beryl,' she said quietly.

'We're not engaged either,' he told her.

'Perhaps not, but I think she's still in your heart. If so, I'll be glad to be friends with you, Jim, but that's all. We could be good companions, but don't try putting me in Beryl's place ... I'm sorry, Jim. I shouldn't have said that, but I was a little ... annoyed.'

He was silent for a time, then he laughed a little.

'At least I know where I stand with you!'

'Which is a good rule for friendship.'

'Then we stay friends?'

She smiled happily. 'We stay friends.'

Again she was surprised when Jim drew her into his arms and kissed her lightly. 'You're a nice girl,' he told her, but this time Jenny drew away, a trifle depressed.

'We'd better go, Jim. Cars keep passing and someone is going to recognise us. Lethansea will be having us engaged if we aren't careful!'

He nodded and started the car. They drove home in silence, and Jenny got out of the car outside the cottage.

'Goodnight, then, Jim.'

'See you soon,' he promised her.

From the direction of The Whins, she could see Robin closing the garage doors, and walking down to close the double wrought-iron gates. He didn't acknowledge her presence, and she wondered a trifle uncomfortably if this had been one of the cars which had passed her and Jim while they had stopped in the lay-by.

It didn't really matter, anyway, she thought dispiritedly. Soon she would only have one term left in Lethansea. Except for Beattie, no doubt people would forget all about her.

7

Jenny's evenings began to be busy, as well as her days. There were rehearsals for the concert, and preparation work to give her children to encourage them in the making of Christmas gifts and cards.

The nativity play was coming on well, and was going to be shown to the parents, along with a display of work done by the children.

Adam Paterson had also formed a small choir from among the older children, and the choir would sing at the concert. Jenny was kept busy playing for them during rehearsals. They were singing one or two traditional Christmas carols, and including 'Linden Lea,' especially for Mrs. Maxwell. The older woman had called in at the school one day with this request.

'I could hear the children singing,'

she explained to Jenny, 'and I'm not ashamed to say that their young voices have given me a lump in my throat. There is so much charm and purity in the voices of children that makes me want to be a better woman.'

Jenny thought that Mrs. Maxwell was a fine woman already, but she nodded, knowing very well what she meant.

'Do you think they could sing 'Linden Lea'?' she asked, rather shyly, 'especially for me?'

'I don't see why not,' agreed Jenny. 'It's one of my favourites, too, and I'm sure Mr. Paterson won't mind.'

'Thank you, dear,' said Mrs. Maxwell, and went away rather quickly.

Perhaps because of this, Jenny had taken special pains in helping to train the sweet young voices, and the result delighted her. She looked forward with pride to their performance, and thought how satisfying it was to be able to do this. Often she would remember the girl who had been doing it before

156

her, and it was as though she knew, instinctively, how Beryl McLean must have felt about it all. It seemed odd to her that she felt she knew the other girl so well, yet they had never met.

She often clung to this feeling when dealing with little Steven, who, she felt, was beginning to accept her and trust her. Often she surprised a look of interest and pleasure on the child's face, and he would laugh with delight along with the other children when she read an amusing story to the class. Jenny was good at reading to children, and if she was obliged to growl like a bear, she growled, much to the delight of the little ones.

Often a sudden remark, or even a reference to Miss McLean, would bring the wooden look back to Steven's face, and Jenny would begin to feel rather tired. It was her one great wish that this little boy would be as happy as any other in the class by the time she again handed over the reins to Beryl. She felt this to be a challenge which she must meet. A child like Steven must not grow up too dependent on his young aunt, and she was determined to encourage the child to be self-reliant before the other girl came home again.

Jenny was getting to know several other people in Lethansea, and to be excited by the talent she found there. Old Joe McMillan, a fisherman all his life, was wonderfully blessed with a deep, rich bass voice.

'You must use it to lure the fish into the boat,' Jenny teased him, admiring his vivid blue eyes which shone fiercely from a face the colour of mahogany.

Joe pushed back his cap and rumpled his silvery curls.

'Or turn them away, miss,' he returned with a twinkle. 'You should ask my brother and my nephew!'

Miss Ellen McGill, who had been the district nurse for many years and was now retired, enchanted Jenny with her 'readings.' It was like the magic of the spoken word to hear her perfect diction as she read a poem which Jenny had known well for years, but which she seemed to be hearing for the first time.

Busy though she was, however, Jenny had time to notice that she wasn't seeing much of Robin Maxwell, and wondered if he was avoiding her. Perhaps he had only been solicitous of her in case she was lonely, and now that she had plenty to do, and had made more friends, he was leaving her alone.

Jenny pondered over this and thought that it was sensible. She ought now to be satisfied with what she had got, and not want to bother Robin, but she couldn't help wanting to see him again, and talk to him a little. But now the long shiny car often swept past the window, and Robin forgot to peer in and acknowledge her presence with a wave.

Jenny remembered that Mrs. Maxwell had invited her to come over any time, and felt that she would like to take advantage of that invitation. Yet . . . her cheeks grew hot at the idea . . . would it seem as though she was chasing Robin? She shied away from that idea, and for a few days she did nothing.

Then one quiet evening she laid aside some exercise books she had been correcting and decided that she would like to go and see the Maxwells again. This time she did have an excuse, as several problems had come up over the concert, and Mrs. Maxwell could soon put them right. Besides, Robin had just gone out in his car, and Jenny was sure that it was only the warm homey atmosphere of The Whins that she wanted to experience again. It had nothing whatever to do with Robin.

Nevertheless she went upstairs and put on a burnt orange-coloured kilt with jersey to match, and clipped a pair of Victorian topaz ear-rings on to her small pink ears.

Her hair was beginning to look very pretty. Repeated cuttings had encouraged it to grow like a smooth cap round her head, and Jenny felt quite pleased with her own appearance.

Beattie thought she looked well, too, when she walked downstairs. In fact, she was so taken with Miss Duff settled down and happy, and Beattie's on it, but found herself with surprisingly little to say.

'I'm only going to see Mrs. Maxwell,' Jenny told her, slipping on her thick woollen coat against the chill of the evening. 'I won't be long, Beattie.'

'Very good, Miss Duff.'

Beattie watched her go, and could hardly believe it was the same girl who had come to her in the late summer. She had thought her a very plain little thing then, but this new girl had an attractive elfin quality about her, a sort of grace, which Beattie found even more compelling than some of the beauties she knew. There were plenty of lovely girls in Lethansca, but Miss Duff was different. She would remember what she looked like long after she had gone back to Glasgow.

Beattie watched her walk over to the Maxwells, noting by the gates that Mr. Robin wasn't at home. Her expression was very thoughtful, those thoughts very busy. It would be a fine thing, though, to see Miss Duff settled down and happy, and Beattie's thoughts turned to the young man from Glasgow. He had seemed a nice enough man, but not the one for Miss Duff. He hadn't come back to eat his tea, after being invited. That wasn't proper behaviour, whatever the reason.

* * *

Mrs. Maxwell was delighted to see Jenny and welcomed her warmly into the sitting-room, which was comfortably untidy.

'Sit down, dear, in front of this fire. You don't know how much pleasure it gives me to see you. I was just feeling I'd welcome a little bit of company.'

'I am glad,' Jenny told her frankly.

'I . . . I was a bit lonely, too.'

'I'll just put on the kettle,' her hostess said happily. 'Robin has gone to see the plant manager about something. They had a small setback last week, you know. I think there was a power failure.'

'Oh dear,' said Jenny. 'Does that mean a lot of alginate was spoiled?'

'I don't think so . . . not really spoiled. I think, though, that it might have to be used for a different purpose than it was originally intended. Robin speaks a lot about his work, though I don't always take it in,' said Mrs. Maxwell, rather ruefully. 'I know I ought to concentrate more, because it's important to him, but I'm getting an older woman now.'

'I thought it was a wonderful industry,' said Jenny, 'when Robin showed me round. I mean, it gives work to the crofters who no doubt need it, and provides further employment round here. It's also a valuable export, and it can be used for so many products. No wonder Robin is so proud to be part of it.'

'Yes, he is proud of it,' agreed Mrs. Maxwell, sitting down. 'I wish . . . ' She broke off, then glanced at Jenny who was regarding her curiously. 'I'm being foolish,' the older woman told her. 'I was just wishing he could be completely happy, that's all. Robin confides all his problems to me, except, perhaps, the most important ones. I mean his personal feelings. No doubt this is because they concern others besides himself, and he doesn't feel free to talk about it.'

Jenny made no comment, and Mrs. Maxwell sighed rather deeply.

'I feel that he . . . he has grown to care for . . . for someone very deeply, and he isn't truly happy because it may be one-sided.'

Jenny tried to control the colour which rose to her cheeks, and wondered what Mrs. Maxwell would say if she knew she was the last person to confide in. At the same time she hated to think of Robin being hurt by Beryl McLean.

Mrs. Maxwell was looking at her intently, as though she was trying to tell her something. Was she trying to hint that she mustn't take Robin's friendship too seriously, since he was already in love with another girl?

She drew a deep breath and smiled, 'What a pity!'

'Yes.' Mrs. Maxwell drew back, perhaps regretting that she had said so much. 'Robin and Beryl McLean were very good friends, but then she was a great deal in Jim Paterson's company, too. I don't think she and Robin . . . ' She broke off and bit her lip, then leaned over and patted Jenny's hand.

'I'm sorry, Jenny. I was worrying a little before you came in, and it helped to tell you my troubles. I'm getting older, you see. Robin is my only son, and David and I had to wait a long time for him. I'd just like to see him settled before . . . before . . . well . . . '

Jenny's eyes were alarmed. 'You mean . . . ?'

'No, of course not. I'm putting this very badly, but I thought you might understand, since you are now on your own.'

Jenny nodded, enlightened.

'Yes, I do understand,' she said quietly, 'but I honestly don't think you need to worry about Robin. I think if he wants something . . . someone . . . very badly, he won't give up very easily.'

'Quite right, and I should have seen that for myself.' For some reason Mrs. Maxwell seemed to be very relieved and smiled on Jenny with satisfaction. 'Now, dear, you said you needed some advice about the concert. What was it you wanted to ask?'

'It's about the encores,' said Jenny, producing her copy of the provisional programme. 'I should be asking Willie Reid. He plays reels and strathspeys on his violin, and we've managed that very well, but I see here it says 'Doodle'.'

'Oh, that!' laughed Mrs. Maxwell. 'Willie can also doodle some Irish tunes . . . like this.'

Mrs. Maxwell gave a spirited imitation of Willie Reid, and Jenny couldn't keep her laughter to herself.

They were both still chuckling when Robin walked in the door.

'Hello, you two, what's the joke?' he asked.

'We were just sorting out problems for the concert,' his mother informed him. 'Jenny and I have been entertaining each other. Will you have some tea, Robin?'

'Later,' he decided. 'I had a cup with Davie Martin.'

There was an awkward silence as he sat down, and Jenny felt that a barrier had grown up between them. Whatever had happened to upset Robin since she was last in his company, it had made him distrustful of her friendship as well.

She caught Mrs. Maxwell's eyes and realised why Robin's mother had, indeed, been anxious about him, and glad to talk it over. Something had happened to bring unhappiness to Robin Maxwell.

The silence was no longer companionable in the lovely room which Jenny admired so much. Last time she had come here to tea, she had felt so much part of it that it had tugged at her heart-strings. Now she felt rather out of it, and rose uncertainly.

'I'd better go now, Mrs. Maxwell,' she said politely. 'I . . . I've enjoyed the evening very much.'

'Do come again, dear,' her hostess insisted, bringing her coat which Robin hastily held for her. She noticed, however, that he didn't second his mother's invitation, nor did he offer to see her back to the cottage.

'Goodnight, then,' Jenny said, making for the door.

'Goodnight, Jenny dear. Will you be all right going across the road? Robin . . . ?'

'I'll be quite all right,' said Jenny

hastily. 'It's only a few yards.'

She hurried into the darkness, and almost ran home. What had happened to Robin? She wondered. It couldn't really be herself who had upset him . . . she didn't mean enough to him for that. No, it must be something else . . . Beryl, for instance? Had he heard from her, and the letter wasn't to his liking?

Jenny pondered, and decided that this was probably the reason for his ill temper.

* * *

By the following weekend Jenny was looking forward to going to Glasgow, and to seeing Charles again. Perhaps, due to the excitement of Christmas ahead, her class had been easier to manage and interested in the projects she planned for them. Even little Steven seemed brighter and happier, and looking forward eagerly to Christmas.

Jenny had given the older children a

small story to write, telling what they liked most about Christmas, and had given them a few ideas.

'You can write about Christmas morning, and the presents you may find in your stocking. Or perhaps Christmas dinner, or even the arrival of the postman with pretty cards from your friends, of maybe going to church and singing carols.'

She had watched Steven take up his pencil as eagerly as anyone, and had been happily surprised when he read his story to find he had a gift for words, and gave a very clear picture of the Christmas he hoped to spend, from opening his cards and gifts to pulling crackers.

Jenny put aside the essay thoughtfully with a feeling of thankfulness. Steven really did seem better these days, and she wondered if her visit to Westerhouse had, perhaps, borne fruit after the McLeans had time to think. Perhaps she had forced them to notice that all wasn't well with the little boy, and they had now done something about it.

The nativity play was now word-perfect, and rehearsals for the concert too were going well. Jenny felt quite satisfied with her first term at Lethansea as she stepped off the train on Friday evening and Charles hurried forward to meet her, bending down to kiss her cheek.

'Hello, Jenny,' he greeted her, then caught back his words as he looked at her more closely. 'You look . . . look lovely.'

There was a hint of surprise in his voice and Jenny laughed, thanking him for the compliment.

'Mrs. Todd is expecting you,' he said, picking up her weekend bag, 'so we'll go straight there, but I thought we could have a nice day together tomorrow.'

'I've brought a nice big shopping list,' she told him. 'I'm looking forward to going round all my favourite stores again. There are some things I do miss in Lethansea.'

'I guessed you would when the novelty had worn off,' said Charles with satisfaction, and Jenny bit back a hasty denial. There was no use disagreeing with Charles at the start of her weekend break. She hoped, however, that he would allow their relationship to remain on terms of good fellowship only.

Jenny was rather touched when Charles called the following morning and told her the plans he had made for her entertainment.

'I thought you'd prefer to shop on your own,' he suggested, 'though I'll be happy to come with you, if you'd rather.'

'No, thanks, Charles,' she said hastily. 'I do like to shop on my own. You'd just get fed up hanging about, waiting for me.'

'That's what I thought,' he agreed, 'so I wondered if I could call back for you here at about six and we could have a meal out, then go to the theatre. I've got tickets, though if you'd rather see a film, I can soon find someone to take them.'

'No, I'd love that,' she told him happily. 'I shall probably be rather footsore, and I shall enjoy relaxing at the theatre.'

Jenny's shopping list seemed to grow longer as she wandered in and out of the stores and although she felt tired, she enjoyed it nevertheless. She also managed to find a lovely dress to wear at the concert. It was a graceful dress, elegantly cut, in a lovely soft shade of hyacinth, which wouldn't have suited her four months ago, but which now suited her perfectly.

She managed to find small suitable gifts for the Maxwells and the Patersons, and a specially nice gift for Beattie, a lovely Celtic brooch set with polished stones. Charles was a problem since she would have to post his gift, and the thought made her wonder what he was doing for Christmas, and if he would expect her to come back to Glasgow.

The thought jolted her a little, as she realised she had expected to spend Christmas quietly, with Beattie. But suppose Beattie wanted to be with her sister in Girvan? Jenny bit her lip, and suddenly felt the loneliness of having no real family. Firmly she put the thought from her and selected a silk scarf for Charles. That would post very easily, and as far as Christmas was concerned . . . well, no doubt she could spend it on her own quite happily.

She was in good spirits again as she walked beside Charles that evening, back to his favourite restaurant. They were inside before she realised he had once again brought her to the same place as last time, and Jenny found her heart beating faster than usual as she sat down and began to look round at the waitresses.

'Had a good day?' asked Charles. Jenny didn't reply for a moment. 'Did you get your shopping done?' he repeated. 'Is there anything wrong?'

'What? No, no, of course not.' She

looked back at him, guiltily. 'Sorry, Charles. I was thinking. Yes, had a very good day.'

Her eyes strayed again, and suddenly she spotted the dark-haired waitress who had served them before, though this time the girl looked very different. Far from being unsure of herself, this girl was quick and efficient, her dark hair caught neatly at the nape of her neck, and her uniform crisp and fresh. She still looked pale, her face thin with the cheekbones marked, but her eyes were large and bright as they met Jenny's without any sign of recognition.

'What's the matter, Jenny?' Charles was asking.

'It's that girl,' she told him. 'I . . . I thought I recognised her. She served us last time, remember?'

'I shouldn't have brought you here,' said Charles, annoyed. 'I'd forgotten that incident. I'm surprised you haven't, though. You're usually the one to let bygones be bygones.'

'I'm not remembering her inefficiency,'

Jenny assured him. 'Besides, she's a very good waitress now. No . . . she's like the girl whose place I've taken . . . Beryl McLean.'

'I thought you hadn't met her.'

'I haven't. I . . . I've seen her photograph.'

'Then it's probably only a likeness. Isn't the girl in Canada?'

'She's supposed to be,' said Jenny slowly. 'Only . . . well, no one ever seems to hear from her, except her brother.'

'Well, surely he's the only one who should hear from her,' said Charles, feeling that this was unimportant to the evening. 'Why should you worry, anyway?'

Jenny shook her head. She would have to see that photograph again. Unless . . .

'I wonder if we could find out her name,' she said, her eyes following the girl as she walked gracefully through the swing doors.

Charles sighed and turned as their

own waitress appeared.

'My friend thinks she recognises the waitress at the next table,' he said heavily. 'Could we know the young lady's name, please?'

The girl looked surprised, and her eyes swept over Jenny.

'Betty Manson,' she said. 'Do you know Betty, madam? Would you like to speak to her?'

Jenny was smiling with relief as she shook her head.

'Mistaken identity,' she said. 'I'm afraid she isn't the girl I thought. Thank you for telling me her name, though.'

'Sorry she isn't your friend,' the waitress said, and Charles looked at her levelly.

'Now can we enjoy our meal?' he asked. 'I hope you've got rid of the bee in your bonnet.'

'Sorry Charles. Yes, I've got rid of it, and I'm glad. It was worrying me quite a bit, off and on. They look terribly alike, you know.'

'They'd probably look quite different side by side,' said Charles. 'Even twins aren't exactly alike.'

'That's true.'

Jenny gave herself up to the enjoyment of the evening, and she was grateful to Charles that, when he saw her home, he only kissed her cheek as a brief goodnight.

'I'll call for you tomorrow and help you with your luggage to the station,' he promised.

'Thank you, Charles. You've been very good. Goodnight.'

★ ★ ★

On Sunday Charles suggested that they take a walk past Jenny's house so that she could see it again. She hesitated for a moment, feeling that she didn't really want to see it again until the lease was up. However, Charles was eager for her to see how attractive it looked, and she agreed.

'It's a good solid house,' he remarked,

as they walked past on the pavement. The garden was looking trim, even in winter, and Jenny felt a nostalgic pull at her heart for the happy years she had spent there, as a child, with her parents.

'It looks very well,' she agreed.

'You can look forward to coming home again,' Charles told her comfortably, and again she felt rather irritated. He had said nothing more about marriage, but now she was remembering his remarks about the novelty wearing off. Was he, perhaps, feeling that she would be glad to come back to him?

She was relieved to be back in the train going home to Beattie. It seemed strange that the tiny seaside village already seemed more like home than the large solid house she had just left behind.

Beattie loved being shown all the things Jenny had brought home for Christmas, although there were one or two packages quickly hidden. The dress, too, was a big success.

'You'll look lovely in that, Miss Duff,' she told her happily. 'I'll be fair proud of you.'

'Thank you, Beattie.'

Jenny's heart was warm. It was so nice to have somebody proud of her.

That evening Jean Paterson walked over to see her, inviting her to the schoolhouse on Christmas Day.

'I wondered whether you'd be going home to Glasgow or not?' she inquired. 'If not, Adam and I would be delighted to have you. Jim usually comes for Christmas dinner, too.'

'How nice of you,' said Jenny, delighted at the prospect. 'Just a moment till I have a word with Beattie. If she's going to be here on her own, then I must ask to be excused.'

But Beattie was also delighted with the arrangement.

'I always go to my sister's on Christmas Day,' she explained. 'We can have breakfast and open our presents, then I'll leave for Girvan in time for dinner.'

'That will suit me fine,' put in Jean. 'We'll expect you over before twelve, Jenny. It will be a quiet day, but we usually enjoy it.'

'I'll look forward to it,' Jenny told her.

* * *

The concert was a huge success, and Jenny did very well as accompanist. She was glad she'd bought her lovely new dress, especially when she saw Carol and Neil McLean in the front row of the audience. Her eyes met Carol's briefly when she went to take her seat at the piano, but there was no warmth of recognition in the other woman's eyes, and Neil McLean looked as though he had only come out of a sense of duty.

Mrs. Maxwell, looking very regal in dark blue velvet, and wearing a very fine pearl necklace, introduced each artist in turn. Jenny's eyes swept the front row for Robin, but he wasn't in the audience. However, just before the opening number, she saw him slip in the side entrance, and take a seat at the end of the row. Somehow his presence soothed her nerves, even more than seeing the Patersons smiling at her encouragingly, and she settled down to play as well as she had ever played before.

Jenny enjoyed every minute of it, wondering briefly if the talent would have sounded so polished in a large concert hall, but decided that it didn't really matter so long as the charm and enthusiasm was all there.

When Mrs. Maxwell thanked her, at the end, and a large bunch of flowers was handed up amidst enthusiastic applause, Jenny's cheeks were scarlet and her eyes shone as she stepped forward. There were quite a few people in the audience who decided that the new teacher was a really bonny girl, and Robin Maxwell gazed up at her, his face inscrutable, then glanced down to where the Patersons were busy applauding with Jim smiling proudly.

Perhaps only Jenny noticed Robin slipping away, and some of the delight went out of her eyes. Surely he hadn't been bored by it all? Why, even the McLeans looked as though they were glad to be here, and to be part of the community.

Mrs. Maxwell caught her arm as the hall began to empty.

'Have you time to come home with me for a nightcap, dear?' she asked. 'I know it's late, but it would be rather nice.'

Jenny's heart leapt with pleasure, then she remembered Robin slipping away so quietly. He wouldn't welcome her arrival with his mother, when he hadn't come forward to speak to her.

'Er . . . it . . . it's rather late,' she said haltingly. 'I see Beattie waiting for me, so I hope you'll excuse me tonight.'

'Of course,' said Mrs. Maxwell, though there was a flash of disappointment in her eyes. She'd probably wanted to talk it all over, and enjoy it a little while longer, and this Jenny found rather touching.

'But I'd like to come and see you soon, if I may,' she said impulsively.

'I was hoping you could spare an hour or two on Christmas Day, but I expect you'll be going to your friends in Glasgow?'

'No, the Patersons have asked me,' said Jenny. 'I'm going to the school-house on Christmas Day, but I'll do my best to call in and wish you the compliments of the season.'

'Oh, that will be nice, Jenny.'

Mrs. Maxwell glanced to where Jim Paterson was obviously hanging about, waiting for a word with Jenny.

'Well, I won't keep you. It's been a splendid evening. Thank you for your help, my dear.'

'I've enjoyed it,' said Jenny sincerely.

★ ★ ★

The nativity play, put on two days later, was not quite so enjoyable from Jenny's point of view, though she was heartened to see so many young parents making time to come and encourage their children. There was one notable exception, she thought, looking round the people gathered in the school hall. The McLeans hadn't bothered to come and see Steven as the Archangel Gabriel. Jenny frowned, wishing that his mother at least had spared a little time. It helped a great deal when parents took an active interest in their children's school work.

However, the little boy didn't seem to mind too much. He had been much happier recently, and Jenny felt very thankful.

The play was the last school event before the holidays, and she felt oddly tired when she prepared to go home. That was one term over, and no doubt the next one would flash past just as quickly now that the children had accepted her, and she had grown accustomed to the work.

Jenny felt a touch of satisfaction, however, as she looked round the empty classroom after the children had gone home, each carrying a tiny gift-wrapped package from their teacher. It had been a challenging term, but a happy one, too. She felt she was a better person for coming to Lethansea, and it had taught her even more than she had taught the children.

Gently Jenny closed the door and went home.

8

When Jenny returned to school in January, she felt even more refreshed after the Christmas break, which she had enjoyed a great deal. She had even managed to put her friendship with Robin back on to a better footing. He had called to see her on Christmas Eve, bringing a small gift for her and Beattie from his mother and himself.

'How lovely,' said Jenny, as she opened her bottle of perfume, which was light and flowery, one of her favourites. 'How nice of you, Robin. Can I thank your mother, too?'

'Why not?' he asked. 'In fact, can't you spare an hour now, or is that booked as well as tomorrow?'

She looked at him quietly.

'I'm quite free, Robin. I'd be delighted to come and see Mrs. Maxwell. Can you wait a moment?

I've got something to bring.'

The 'something' was a small gift each for Robin and Mrs. Maxwell, but Jenny carried them in a paper bag as she walked beside him over to The Whins.

'Oh, how nice!'

Mrs. Maxwell bent and kissed her cheek, while Jenny thanked her shyly for the gifts, then produced her own, watching with pleasure while Mrs. Maxwell admired a dainty little china ornament and Robin opened a book he had once mentioned as one he would like to read.

'Fancy you remembering!' he exclaimed, obviously delighted.

Jenny coloured, and avoided his eyes.

'I . . . I just sort of . . . remembered . . . ' she said, lamely.

She could hardly explain that everything Robin had ever told her was as clear as crystal in her memory.

When Mrs. Maxwell disappeared into the kitchen, there was an awkward silence between them.

'Jenny, I . . . ' began Robin, and stopped as she, too, began to speak.

'I hope I haven't offended you, Robin. I . . . I thought, recently, you were avoiding me, and I'm sorry if I've said anything to upset you. I valued you as a friend.'

Robin's face had grown pale, but now his eyes softened and he reached over for his pipe before turning to her.

'I'm sorry, Jenny, if I seemed rather moody. It was nothing . . . nothing at all. Certainly it wasn't your fault. Of course we're friends, and we'll keep it that way.'

'I am glad, Robin,' she said happily.

He leapt to his feet to help his mother with the tray and Jenny again felt the warmth and charm of being part of this family as they sat round the fire and talked happily together. For a moment she regretted that she would be going to the schoolhouse next day. How much nicer it would be if only she were coming here! Then she felt ashamed. The Patersons had been very good to her, and Jim was another good friend. She ought to be very grateful to them for their kind invitation.

Nevertheless, it was with reluctance that she again rose from the cosy fireside, and told Mrs. Maxwell she ought to be going home.

'I hope you have a lovely Christmas tomorrow,' she said shyly.

'Thank you, Jenny, but I always think it's the happiest time of all with children in the house. Now, if I'd only had some grandchildren, what a happy day it would be!'

Jenny saw the guarded look coming back on to Robin's face.

'I'll walk back with you, Jenny,' he offered, and helped her into her coat.

This time he took her arm, firmly, and they walked in silence.

'Merry Christmas, Jenny, when it comes,' he said softly, and bent to kiss her.

Jenny felt the warm colour again

steal into her cheeks, but her voice was casual.

'Merry Christmas, Robin.'

She mustn't misinterpret a Christmas kiss. It was meant to seal the bargain on their friendship, but Jenny's heart stayed warm for a long time.

★ ★ ★

Christmas Day was spent quietly and pleasantly with the Patersons doing all they could to make it a happy day for her. Jim was rather quiet and flushed a little when Adam asked if he had had a card from Beryl.

'No,' he said shortly.

'The post from Canada is very uncertain,' Jean assured him. 'I've often heard of Christmas parcels arriving at the end of January.'

Jim laughed rather harshly.

'I'm not expecting any parcel,' he said. 'I rather think Beryl is finding her new life all-absorbing. If it weren't for Neil, I'd think she'd vanished into thin air, but he's just had a letter from her saying she was having a wonderful time. He took the trouble to tell me so when I saw him the other day. She only seems to find time to write to her own family.'

He turned to Jenny.

'If you like Lethansea, you might even be given the opportunity of making that job permanent, Jenny.'

'Don't go saying that,' said Adam quickly. 'Jenny has come here under a temporary arrangement. If there's to be any change, it will be discussed through the proper quarters, and won't be anything to do with you, Jim.'

'Sorry,' he said. 'It was just that . . . Oh, well, never mind. Come on and let's play that game we found in my cracker.'

'Yes, let's,' said Jean, with obvious relief. 'We can sit round this small table.'

Soon all four were laughing as they played the simple game, but Jenny often glanced at Jim, feeling the hidden tension in him. How could Beryl neglect him so much if they had been good friends? She must have known that it went deeper with Jim, since it was so easy to see he was in love with her. Now that he had lost all contact with her, it must be very frustrating.

Jenny left the schoolhouse early that evening, feeling she would like to spend a quiet hour with Beattie, watching television, then off to bed. It had been an unusual Christmas for her, with lots of pretty gifts including a silver bracelet from Charles.

'I could have wished this to be a different piece of jewellery, but it comes to you with my love.'

Jenny felt rather touched, but wished that Charles had chosen a simpler gift, more like the pretty scarf from Jim or the perfume from Robin.

In another week there would be the promise of a New Year, though Jenny felt that there were some rocks ahead. There were still many problems to solve in her own life, and in the lives of new friends she had come to love.

★ ★ ★

Her one big disappointment was the fact that she couldn't attend the Hogmanay Dance. She'd walked slowly and thoughtfully along the sea-front a couple of days after Christmas, trying to clear her thoughts which were disturbed, oblivious of the cold wetness of the marshy grass.

'You'll get your death,' Beattie admonished her when she returned home. 'Get out of those wet boots and stockings, and you'd better rub down your legs and have a hot bath. Whatever were you thinking about, Miss Duff?'

Jenny sighed. It was very pleasant to be fussed over, and she relaxed in front of the fire and drank a large mug of cocoa. But it hadn't prevented the heavy head cold which made her nose feel twice its size and her eyes water.

'I can't go to the dance like this,' she told Beattie.

'Maybe you'll feel better tomorrow,' the older woman encouraged her.

'Maybe,' said Jenny sceptically.

Both Robin and Jim called to see her, and Jenny could scarcely hide her disappointment. It would have been her first big dance in Lethansea, and she had been looking forward to dancing with Robin. And Jim, too, she told herself hastily.

However, Beattie agreed that it would be very unwise for Jenny to do anything but stay in and nurse her cold, and she wiped her streaming eyes and agreed.

She must be quite better for the start of the new term, and in fact, the rest did her good, and she went back to school with renewed enthusiasm.

It was a delight for Jenny to see all her small pupils again, though when her eyes swept the class, she found that Steven was missing, and hoped he wasn't ill.

A quarter of an hour later, however,

there was a knock on the classroom door, and Jenny hurried to open it to find Carol McLean staring at her, rather haughtily, clasping Steven by the hand. The little boy was white-faced and hung back, unwilling to look at Jenny.

'Perhaps you can explain why he refuses to come to school, Miss Duff,' Carol said, with annoyance. 'He's been more difficult than ever over Christmas, and now he's using every excuse under the sun to get out of coming back to school.'

She stared at Jenny, obviously blaming her for this reluctance on Steven's part, and Jenny knelt down beside the small boy.

'Is there anything worrying you, dear?' she asked gently. 'Can we take off your coat and you can go and sit with your friends in your usual place? If there's anything at all that you don't understand, don't worry about it. I'll explain it to you again, so that you'll be able to understand it easily.'

She took the child's arm, but he almost flung her away, and Jenny's face paled when she met Carol's eyes.

'There you are,' the older girl said triumphantly. 'I really think I ought to see Mr. Paterson and make fresh arrangements for Steven. Obviously he's afraid of you in some way, Miss Duff. I've been wondering how you discipline your class. Steven has never been this difficult before.'

Jenny's eyes flashed.

'I'm an experienced teacher, Mrs. McLean,' she said quietly. 'I don't think you'd have any complaints about my discipline from any other child in the class. I've been worried about Steven for some time, which is why I came to see you. But if you'd like to talk it over with Mr. Paterson . . .'

'I'll sit in the class,' said Steven, suddenly and clearly. 'I'll sit beside Tommy and Ian.'

He took off his coat and handed it to his mother, then went quietly to his place. Carol McLean looked nonplussed, then she turned again to Jenny.

'I'm by no means satisfied, Miss Duff. I shall have to take this further if Steven gets upset like this. He's a sensitive child.'

'I agree entirely,' Jenny told her crisply. 'I think Steven really is worried about something, and I would be happy to co-operate with you to find out what it is. At the moment, however, I have other children waiting.'

Carol McLean's lips pressed together, then she sailed off down the corridor, hanging Steven's coat on a peg as she went past. Jenny went back to her class, and tried to collect her thoughts. She decided to accept Steven's presence back in his usual place without comment, and began her normal programme of work. But her mind was busy. Somehow or other she must get Steven McLean to tell her what was troubling him. If it was one of the lessons, then she must be prepared to help him as much as possible.

She felt disquieted. She had been so sure that Steven's upset came from his home background, but now it looked very much as though it lay in the school, and particularly with her. Did he resent her being in his Aunt Beryl's place? Was that why he was being so difficult?

Worried, Jenny had a word with Adam Paterson, who listened to her carefully.

'It could be the first day back at school,' he said thoughtfully. 'I've known other children to take aversion to school work, and make all sorts of excuses to avoid coming back.'

'It could be,' she said doubtfully. 'But you think there's more?'

She nodded. 'I think he'd be more noisy about it if he was just trying to get off school. He'd be ill with a tummy upset or a headache.'

'Shall I have a word with the McLeans, or even the child? I've hesitated to interfere since you seemed to be doing so well with him. Perhaps, even, a word with Neil Prentice. He's a good doctor, with lots of experience . . . '

She debated with herself.

'Perhaps we could give him a day or two to settle down, and if he doesn't, then see his parents. Advise them to have a word with Dr. Prentice.'

'All right, Jenny. I trust your judgement.'

She was grateful. 'Then . . . then you don't think I've been rather incompetent . . . where Steven is concerned, I mean?'

'No, I don't think so at all. I do keep out of your way, Jenny, but that doesn't mean I haven't been interested, or haven't watched how you work. I'm perfectly satisfied, my dear.'

'Thank you.'

Jenny felt much better, but she went home in a very anxious frame of mind. In spite of Adam Paterson's encouraging words, she couldn't forget the accusing look on Carol McLean's face or the way little Steven shook off her hand when she took his arm.

Was she, in some way, to blame for the child's upset? What could she have done to destroy his trust in her?

Jenny worried herself, and Beattie gave her more than one speculative look, but knew when to hold her tongue. Miss Duff wasn't slow to confide in her when she needed advice. Obviously this was something which she wanted to resolve on her own.

Nevertheless she was still worrying about Jenny when she went over to see Mrs. Maxwell about a sale of work being organised for the church. Beattie had been asked to knit some 'beehive' tea-cosies, and Mrs. Maxwell had spare wool which she thought would suit the purpose.

'She's a bit peaky,' Beattie confided, having been asked how Jenny was keeping after her cold. 'Either she's not picking up, or . . . or something.' Beattie was torn between being indiscreet and getting help for her young lady. She saw Robin looking at her, and knew he was the very one to take Jenny out of herself. 'She's not herself,' she finished firmly. 'Not herself at all.'

'I'll go over and see her,' said Robin, rising.

But Jenny wasn't at all pleased to have Robin calling on her just because Beattie had noticed she 'wasn't herself'. She didn't want him to bother with her out of a sense of duty.

'I'm all right, Robin,' she protested.

'Beattie says you aren't,' he told her flatly. 'Don't get yourself run down. You ... you're such a little thing that I often wonder if you've much stuffing.'

It wasn't quite what Jenny wanted to hear, though she could see now that Robin was concerned for her.

'Come, Jenny,' he said, suddenly gentle. 'Is there anything wrong? Can't I help, or is it something very private?'

'Not so very, no.'

'Then ... can't I help?'

Tears stung at the gentleness in his voice.

'No, really, it's ... it's all right.

I'm just getting adjusted again, back at school, and some problems have cropped up.'

'I see.'

Robin slowly filled his pipe, and observed her carefully, waiting to hear if she'd anything more to say. But Jenny felt that the only way he could help with Steven would be to tell her more about the McLeans, and especially about Beryl.

She looked at him, seeing his dark auburn hair glowing in the firelight, and the dark freckles on his face. She knew now that she loved him very much, and would always love him, but she felt she couldn't question him about Beryl McLean, the girl whom he might, in fact, love. She didn't want to hear him talk about the other girl, and no doubt he wouldn't wish to discuss her anyway.

'I don't think you can help, Robin,' she told him evenly. 'I think I'll have to work it out for myself.'

'Very well, Jenny,' he nodded, though

some of the warmth had left his voice.

'Please . . . don't be offended,' she said quickly. 'I . . . ' She broke off, wondering how she could explain.

'Can't Adam Paterson help you?'

'Oh yes. Yes, of course.'

There was an awkward silence, then Robin stood up.

'I'm going to a wee place called Barr on Saturday. Come with me,' he invited.

'Where's that?'

'In-country from Girvan.'

Jenny nodded, her eyes on his face. 'All right. Thank you.'

'Problems have a habit of working themselves out,' he told her, then grinned almost to himself. 'How I wish I believed that!'

She didn't smile.

'Cheer up,' he told her, and pressed a finger to her small nose. 'See you Saturday.'

Beattie arrived home half an hour later and looked doubtfully at Jenny.

'We're going out on Saturday,' said

Jenny, 'to Barr. Robin is taking me out of myself.'

'That's good,' said Beattie, satisfied.

★ ★ ★

Jenny was glad of the purposed trip to Barr during the following week It was something to look forward to when she felt rather depressed and worried by little Steven McLean.

She hated to see the look of wooden acceptance back on his face, and when some of the children told her all about their Christmas break, he had nothing at all to say.

Tommy McIver, who sat next to Steven, was more forthcoming.

'I got roller skates,' he said proudly, 'and a jigsaw and a big train set.'

'That's lovely, Tommy,' Jenny told him, smiling. 'What about you, Steven?'

The child looked at her stonily.

'He got a bicycle from his mum and dad, and a racing car set from Miss McLean,' Tommy said helpfully.

'Those are splendid gifts,' said Jenny, as the class filed out to go to the cloakroom.

'But he doesn't like his car set,' Tommy added, 'He wanted a real Indian outfit with real feathers.'

This time Steven's face grew red and his mouth crumpled.

'I didn't!' he said fiercely. 'I only pretended I did. I only pretended.'

Jenny quickly knelt beside the little boy. Was this the answer? she wondered. Had he been disappointed in some way?

'Didn't you like your car set or bicycle?' she asked gravely.

His small mouth pouted. 'It's all right,' he told her sullenly.

'It's a lovely gift,' Jenny told him, 'and especially nice when it's come a long way. Lots of little boys would love gifts like that.'

'She just gave it to Mummy and Daddy for me,' said Steven mulishly, 'and she promised . . . '

For a moment he swallowed, then

turned away and joined the other children who were struggling into their coats.

'He was going to have given me the stamp off his Christmas card,' said Tommy, looking almost as mulish as Steven. 'It was for my stamp collection.'

Jenny went back to her desk, very thoughtful. It seemed very odd that a splendid teacher like Beryl McLean had broken her promise to a child, and especially her nephew. Or could it be that Carol and Neil McLean had given Steven the car set from Beryl so that he wouldn't be disappointed on Christmas Day? Perhaps they had no idea that the child was hurt by what he thought was a broken promise.

Jenny turned the question over and over in her mind, and resolved to go again to Westerhouse and talk this over with the McLeans. A quiet pointer in the right direction might save endless worry to the child, if only he could have immediate reassurance that his

Aunt Beryl hadn't deliberately broken her promise. In fact, the longed-for Indian outfit might easily still be in the post.

After tea Jenny again put on her heavy coat and boots, then made her way along the now familiar road to Westerhouse.

The young girl who answered the door when she rang the bell told her that Mrs. McLean was not at home.

'Mr. McLean, then,' Jenny insisted, seeing his car sitting in the drive. 'I'd be most grateful if Mr. McLean could spare me five minutes of his time.'

The girl asked her to wait in the hall, then went and knocked lightly on one of the doors and went into the room. Jenny could hear the low murmur of their voices, and a moment later she was asked to step inside.

The room was a man's room, with a large mahogany desk, deep leather chairs and well-filled bookshelves. Neil McLean had been working at his desk, and looked up tiredly and rather coldly when Jenny walked into the room.

'I'm very busy, Miss . . . er . . . Duff,' he told her heavily. 'My wife usually deals with any problems which come up with regard to Steven.'

'I won't keep you longer than I can help, Mr. McLean,' Jenny told him quietly. 'I wouldn't have come if I hadn't considered it important.'

For a moment there was a flash of concern in Neil McLean's tired eyes.

'Of course,' he said. 'Please sit down and tell me how I can help you.'

'Steven hasn't settled down since Christmas,' Jenny told him flatly. 'You probably know that he didn't want to come back to school.'

'I know he's a normal boy for his age,' Neil McLean said carefully. 'Few boys like Steven enjoy going back to school after the freedom of a holiday.'

'This was rather more than that sort of reluctance,' Jenny told him, 'but I have got an idea what is troubling him, and I'm sorry if I must touch on personal matters. I understand, though, that he was disappointed over his gift from your sister, Miss McLean, because he'd been promised an Indian outfit . . .'

'He got a gift from my sister,' said Neil McLean, coldly, 'and really, Miss Duff, I fail to see why it should be your concern . . .'

'I know. A car set,' went on Jenny bravely, her face growing hot. 'I . . . I rather think that the Indian outfit was very precious to him since it was coming from Canada, and therefore 'real' to him. Children often set their hearts on things like that . . .'

Neil McLean's face had gone rather hard. 'Have you questioned Steven about this, Miss Duff?' he asked sharply.

'No . . . no . . . but he's definitely unhappy about this gift. As a matter of fact it was his little friend, Tommy McIver, who gave me a clue, otherwise I might never have known what was wrong. Mr. McLean . . . I know it seems unforgivable of me to interfere in this way, but if the Indian outfit is likely to be in the post . . . I mean, if you bought the car set so that you didn't want to disappoint the little boy, couldn't you . . . ?'

'Miss Duff, I suppose I ought to be grateful to you for the interest you take in my son, but I really think you are taking it a little too far. I'd be more concerned if Steven himself had told you he was upset over Christmas, but it appears to have come from another child.'

'But . . . ' Jenny bit her lip. There was something immovable about Neil McLean, as though he didn't want to hear anything more about Steven. Jenny looked at him, wondering how a man could become so wrapped up in his business that he had no time to take a proper interest in his little boy. He ought to be listening to what she had to say, and weighing it up from all possible angles. Surely he couldn't be so blind as not to see that Steven wasn't himself.

Jenny met his eyes squarely, and saw them flicker again, almost as though he were afraid. Then she turned to pick up her bag, telling herself that she was becoming imaginative. Why on earth would Neil McLean be afraid of her?

'I'm sorry to have troubled you,' she said huskily, and watched him hesitate.

'Please don't think I don't appreciate what you're trying to do,' he said, with difficulty, 'only I . . . ' Again he hesitated. 'I'm sure Steven will be quite all right,' he said firmly. 'Some children have more difficulty growing up than others. Steven is a sensitive child, but he'll be all right, Miss Duff.'

'Of course,' she said quickly. 'Don't come to the door, Mr. McLean. I'll see myself out.'

Yet she was irritated and dissatisfied as she walked down the path. Her visit had accomplished nothing again, and she couldn't agree that Steven's behaviour was that of an ordinary little boy, slow to adjust.

'If only his Aunt Beryl would send that Indian outfit!' she thought fiercely. That might help quite a lot.

That night Jenny remembered the Christmas card, and Tommy's disappointment over the stamp. Surely Beryl had sent her small nephew a card, and it was more than likely that a card would arrive in time for Christmas, even if a parcel was late.

Jenny turned the thought over in her mind, and doubts began to crowd in on her again. There was something about Beryl McLean's visit to Canada which made her feel very uneasy. If she was really enjoying her holiday there, then why hadn't she written to her friends back home? Why hadn't she kept Steven well posted with even small things which would delight him?

Yet, if she had changed her mind about the visit, why should Neil McLean pretend everything was all right?

Jenny felt she didn't know enough about Neil McLean to judge, and her thoughts turned to Jim Paterson who knew Neil very well. Would it be possible to find out Jim's opinion of Neil by asking one or two careful questions?

Jenny frowned and bit her lip. She'd feel like a spy, she thought with distaste, then the thought of little Steven's pale face rose in her mind's eye. She didn't seem to be helping much by being straightforward about everything. Suppose she tried something different. She would call in at the Patersons' the following evening and see if she could talk to Jim.

But Jim wasn't with the Patersons when Jenny called, and Jean invited her in, warmly welcoming.

'Do come in, Jenny,' she said. 'We haven't seen so much of you since school started again.'

'Er . . . no . . . I'm sorry,' the younger girl said apologetically. 'I've been rather busy in the evenings.'

'Jim will be here on Saturday,' Jean

told her. 'Suppose you come round then.'

'No, I'm going out on Saturday,' said Jenny, with a laugh. 'I've promised to go out with Robin. To Barr, I think.'

Jean's eyebrows raised a little, and Jenny felt annoyed by the blush which crept up her cheeks.

'He only thought I'd like a change,' she said, rather defensively.

'You'll enjoy it,' Jean told her. 'It's all right, Jenny, I'm not trying to tease you.'

Jenny's eyes lit up in a smile.

'I know. I'll see Jim some time, then. It isn't terribly urgent.'

She left the schoolhouse to walk back home, her thoughts busy. Perhaps it was just as well that Jim wasn't available. She wasn't the type to go pumping anyone, and would only make a mess of it, and probably succeed in passing on her disquiet to Jim.

★ ★ ★

It was after dinner on Saturday when Robin called for Jenny, and waited while she put on her warm woolly coat in a soft shade of amber which brought a warm flush to her pale cheeks and made her eyes glow.

'Put on a scarf, too,' he advised. 'It can be cold in the country, though we're lucky with the weather at the moment.'

'All right, Robin,' she agreed meekly.

Beattie fussed over her a little, obviously pleased to see her taking some time off for the outing.

'We won't be late back,' said Jenny as she walked to the car, 'will we, Robin?'

'Expect us when you see us, Beattie,' he grinned, and a moment later they were taking the Girvan road.

'I want to visit a man I know through my work who has had an accident and injured his leg,' he explained to Jenny as they sped along the clear straight road. 'He's married, and I'm sure his wife will be delighted to make you welcome while John and I talk business, though if you don't feel too sociable today, there are plenty of nice walks round the village. It's a pretty place with a fine fishing river running through it, and it nestles among the hills'

'How long would you be?' asked Jenny, who decided that Robin might feel freer to attend to business on his own. Besides, a brisk walk in the clear fresh air, exploring a pretty new village, might be just what she needed.

'About an hour, I should think,' he told her, 'then I thought we could go for a run round the hills, and back to Girvan for tea. Perhaps even the pictures if you feel like a night out.'

Jenny thought she would enjoy that very much as she settled down to look at the lovely freshness of the countryside, even in winter.

'I used to hate winter,' she told Robin, 'but this year I'm enjoying it. It's like a time of rest for nature, and I feel as though I've been experiencing a little bit of winter myself.'

'And do you now feel a touch of spring in the air?' he asked, his eyes serious in spite of his teasing voice.

'Not yet,' she confessed, after a long moment.

'Winter doesn't last for ever,' he told her quietly, 'and sometimes it doesn't do to expect too much, of ourselves or anyone else. Things can be easier if we settle for less.'

Jenny nodded, but thought that she couldn't settle for less with regard to little Steven McLean. She'd have to keep trying till she felt sure the child was all right.

'I can't settle for less,' she told Robin, and he glanced briefly at her neat profile.

'No, I don't suppose you can, Jenny,' he said, rather bleakly.

Jenny loved Barr. Robin stopped the car near the river, and gave her a spare key, in case she got tired of walking before he had finished business.

'If you're cold, switch on the engine

and the heater,' he told her, 'or you can listen to the radio.'

'I won't be cold after a good brisk walk,' she laughed.

'Here's a bar of chocolate in case you feel hungry.'

He popped it into her pocket after turning her round and pulling her scarf more firmly round her neck.

Jenny laughed again, then her heart raced a little as her eyes met Robin's and it seemed as though the world stood still between them. Then abruptly he turned away and locked the car door while she pulled on her warm woolly gloves.

'Don't go too far,' he said lightly, 'and don't get lost. We . . . we mustn't lose Jenny.'

Somehow it seemed as though spring had come in spite of the hard ground which sparkled with frost in the pale winter sunshine. Jenny wore warm comfortable boots and she breathed deeply of the fresh hill air as she walked along, admiring the fresh clear river, and the charming little houses clustering together to make a pretty picture. She must come again in summer, she decided, when the gardens would be full of flowers and the country-side lush and green.

But would she be here in summer? she wondered, pausing to look down on the village. It was more likely that this would all be just a memory by then, and no longer part of her life.

The thought was painful to her as she walked along, through the quietness of the countryside, and resolutely she put it from her. She must enjoy her day, and store it away among her memories so that it would always be with her.

But it was growing dusk when Robin finally returned to the car.

'Were you all right?' he asked anxiously. 'I wasn't too long, was I?'

'Of course not,' she smiled. 'I enjoyed my walk very much and a nice rest afterwards. I like a little bit of solitude now and again.'

'I've noticed,' he told her, rather dryly. 'I'm afraid it's getting dark for sightseeing, so we'll go on to Girvan and have a meal. Would you like to go to the pictures, or straight home?'

'I'd enjoy a night out,' she said, her eyes shining.

'Good. I feel that way myself!'

'Was . . . was your friend feeling better?' she asked.

'He was at the bored stage,' Robin told her ruefully. 'It isn't easy being compelled to rest when your inclinations are all to the contrary. It can bring out the best, and the worst, in a man.'

There was an edge to his voice, and Jenny glanced at his profile in the gathering dusk. Was Robin feeling thwarted, too?

They found a charming little restaurant and ordered a meal, Jenny finding that she was very hungry after her brisk walk in the fresh air.

'I eat like a horse these days,' she said, laughing.

'Well, it'll be a long time before you

start to look like one,' he returned, eyeing her slender figure, 'though you look very well, Jenny.'

Again she felt her heart leap as Robin reached over and took her hand, gazing at her intently. Surely it couldn't be that Robin . . . that he . . .

'Hello, Jenny! Robin!'

The colour flew to her face as she turned round to see Jim Paterson standing beside their table. A quick glance at Robin's face showed her that Jim wasn't the most welcome of people.

'Nice to see you both,' he was saying happily. 'I'd join you, but I'm with a party of friends. Tom Dallas . . . you remember Tom Dallas, Robin? . . . he and Sally McBride have just got engaged, so we're having a celebration.'

'Then we won't keep you,' said Robin, rather pointedly.

'Oh, it's all right. They won't miss me for just a moment. I wanted a word with Jenny. Jean says you were asking about me the other day, wanting to see me about something?'

Jenny felt her face grow hot while Robin's expression grew rather remote.

'It . . . it was nothing,' she said. 'I . . . I forget what it was.'

'Oh,' said Jim. He looked at them both uncertainly. 'Oh well, that's all right then, Jenny. Sorry I wasn't available at the time. I was meaning to call round and see you this evening after it broke up here.'

'Thank you, Jim,' said Jenny, smiling a little.

'Cheerio, then,' he nodded. 'See you both later.'

'Cheerio,' said Jenny, and Robin nodded.

There was an uncomfortable silence after Jim left and Jenny wondered how she could explain to Robin why she had wanted to talk to Jim Paterson. How could she tell him she had only wanted to ask questions about the McLeans, especially now that the idea was distasteful to her?

Her heart felt rather heavy when she looked at Robin's closed face. For a moment it had seemed that there was something rather wonderful and precious between them, but now it had gone, torn away as though it had never been.

Robin looked at his watch.

'If you still want to go to the pictures, we'd better get a move on,' he said coldly. 'I . . . I hope you don't feel that I'm taking up too much of your time.'

She felt her mouth go rather dry.

'Of course not. I'd love to come, Robin.'

He helped her into her coat, and she walked out into the clear cold night air. Robin grasped her elbow as they crossed the street, but the touch of his fingers was impersonal and he no longer tucked her hand under his arm. Jenny blinked back the tears, then lifted her chin, proudly determined not to allow him to see her heart.

Jenny could hardly have told anyone

what the film was all about. She sat quietly beside Robin and tried to concentrate on the programme, but her own emotions were upset, and she felt that Robin was almost a stranger again, instead of the pleasant companion he had been during the day.

When they left the cinema, Robin again guided her towards the car and helped her into the front seat. It was a clear night, in spite of the chill, and she watched the lights of various lighthouses flashing rhythmically, as the car sped along the coast road home.

'How lovely it is,' she sighed. 'I shall remember nights like this always.'

'And perhaps want to keep them always?' asked Robin.

There was a cool note in his voice and she turned to look at him curiously, uncertain how to answer.

'Our lives don't always follow the pattern we want,' she said at last.

'Very true.'

Then suddenly Robin softened, and there was a gentle note in his voice, this time, as he turned to her.

'Don't mind me, Jenny. I never thought I was a jealous man, and always believed in letting the best man win. That was before I had anything to care about deeply and I find, now, I'm just as bad as the next man. Jealousy isn't a very comfortable emotion. It makes us forget that even our best friends are our best friends.'

'You . . . you mean Jim Paterson?'

'I mean a nice chap like Jim Paterson.'

Jenny didn't know what to say. Was Robin jealous of Jim because of Beryl McLean . . . or . . . or could it be because of her? Surely it couldn't be her! She wanted to ask him, but the words refused to come.

She was aware that the car had stopped and reached quickly for her handbag.

'Goodnight, Robin,' she said hurriedly. 'It was nice of you to take me with you today. I . . . I've enjoyed the break.'

'That's good, Jenny,' he told her,

rather tiredly. 'Goodnight.'

Again she felt restless and dissatisfied as she let herself in with her own key, to find Beattie fussing with some hot milk.

'I don't want it, Beattie,' she said, then felt contrite when she saw the slightly huffed expression on her landlady's face. She had come to love Beattie and wouldn't have hurt her for the world.

'Very well, Miss Duff.'

'No. Can I change my mind, Beattie? I'm very tired, but maybe it would help me to sleep.'

Beattie softened, realising Jenny did, indeed, look tired.

'Here you are,' she said, handing her a steaming mug. 'Drink it down. It'll do you a lot o' good.'

Jenny thought wryly that it would take more than hot milk to soothe her rather sore heart.

9

In the end it was Beattie who told Jenny a little more about the McLeans when she came home from school a few days later.

She was still finding Steven difficult to handle, and that day she had found him in tears, hiding in the cloakroom, though he pulled away from her when she tried to talk to him.

Over tea her mind was full of her problem and she didn't answer when Beattie rambled on a little, giving her small items of local news.

'I . . . I'm sorry, Beattie,' she said, coming out of her thoughts to find a heavy silence in the room, 'did you ask me something?'

'It doesn't matter,' said Beattie, rather stiffly.

'Of course it matters,' Jenny told her. 'It was unforgivable of me not to listen more carefully. It's just that . . . well, I have a problem of my own to solve.'

Beattie sat down and her expression softened.

'I've seen that you were worried for a wee while, Miss Duff,' she acknowledged. 'It . . . it isn't anything I can help you with?'

Jenny shook her head.

'Not really. Just something at school.'

After a long moment she asked,

'Did you know Mr. Neil McLean when he was a boy? I mean, did you know the family at all?'

'My sister knew them,' Beattie told her. 'She used to give a hand with the cleaning at times. Old Mr. McLean was a fine man, and very hard-working.'

'Then it's a good business?'

'Just a small firm . . . coach-building, you know. I don't think they have many workers.'

'I see.'

'There were rumours that Mr. Neil wasn't the man his father was, and didn't make such a good job of running the place. He looks like his father, but that doesn't mean he's like him in nature. Miss Beryl is very like her mother, very soft and gentle. Mrs. McLean was a Manson before she married. Miss Elizabeth Manson from one of the big houses south of here, in Galloway.'

A vague memory tugged at Jenny's mind. Miss Manson. Where had she heard that name before?

'I've heard that name before, Beattie,' she said slowly.

'Do you know someone else of the same name?'

Jenny shook her head slowly.

'No . . . unless it was Mr. Paterson who told me about the McLeans. I think he mentioned that Mrs. McLean was a Manson.'

Jenny put out her cup for more tea when Beattie offered it, pouring it out of her large brown teapot. Suddenly she had a flash of memory, and of herself pouring tea for Charles in a Glasgow restaurant . . . and of asking the waitress the name of the girl with the long dark hair. Betty Manson! Miss Elizabeth Manson.

Jenny felt her mouth go dry, and her heart beat a little more loudly with excitement, though she sat, outwardly calm, turning this new information over in her mind. Was it the same girl?

'Beattie,' she said at length, 'do you remember those photographs you showed me? The ones taken when Miss McLean left?'

Beattie nodded.

'At that do we had to give her a presentation?'

'That's right. Could I see them again, please?'

Beattie lost no time in finding the photographs, and Jenny couldn't stop her fingers trembling when she took them, and gazed again at the lovely girl with the soft dark hair.

It was the same girl! She was sure of it as she gazed at the photograph, her expressive face full of excitement. Beattie looked at her intently.

231

'Do you know Miss McLean?' she asked bluntly. 'I mind when you saw those photographs before, you thought you knew her.'

Jenny hardly knew how to reply.

'I can't say, because I can't be too sure,' she said carefully. 'I think I've seen her before.'

Beattie sat down again, her face rather white.

'It wouldn't be in Glasgow, would it, Miss Duff?'

'Why?'

'Well . . . ' Beattie had difficulty in finding her words, then it all rushed out. 'It was our Janet's eldest boy, who is up in Glasgow, studying to be an accountant. He knew Miss Beryl fairly well, and he swears he saw her in a restaurant in Glasgow, serving at the tables. We all thought he was off his head, since she went off to Canada, not Glasgow. But he's such a reliable boy, and I don't think he'd make a mistake. Miss Duff, I've been fair worried about this, on and off, for a long while . . . ever since a week after she went away, in fact. I just didn't know what to do or if I should mention it to anyone. I mean, why should Miss McLean want to go hiding herself in Glasgow instead of going to her sister's when it was all arranged for her? If she hadn't wanted to go at the last minute, why didn't she just stay at home? It . . . it just doesn't make sense. Not unless . . . '

Beattie went scarlet, then bit her lip.

'Not unless she was hiding from some man, and I don't know anyone in Lethansea she'd need to hide from. I mean . . . Miss Beryl's not the type to run away, if you know what I mean.'

Jenny thought she did, though she didn't put those thoughts into words. Yet now she was absolutely sure it was Beryl McLean she had seen in Glasgow.

They were both silent for a while, then Beattie asked tentatively.

'Did you see her in Glasgow, too?'

'It could have been her double, but now that your nephew has said it was Miss McLean, then I think it was the same girl. He's quite right about the restaurant. That's where I saw her, too.'

'Then . . . what should we do about it? I thought and thought, and kept trying to tell myself it was none of my business what Miss Beryl did. Only maybe that's not quite true. Suppose . . . suppose she's in trouble of some kind and I haven't tried to help. That's what I tell myself. We don't like to interfere with each other too much in Lethansea, but we don't like to see people trying to bear troubles alone either.'

'I know,' said Jenny gently. 'I tell you what I'll do, Beattie. I'll go to Glasgow on Friday night again . . . I can ring up Mrs. Todd, the janitor's wife, and she'll likely have me again for a couple of nights. I'll try to see Miss McLean and find out what it's all about . . .'

'Only if she needs help, Miss Duff,'

put in Beattie firmly.

'Of course, Beattie. Otherwise we leave her alone. But I need her help, if she *is* Beryl McLean. At least, her nephew needs her help. I think that wee soul senses something is wrong, and it's put him in a fine state of nerves. If she'll put things right with Steven, then she can live her life in Glasgow in whatever way suits her. I shan't want to interfere.'

Beattie nodded.

'Will you tell Mr. Cairns you're going?' she asked carefully.

Jenny hesitated, aware of the oblique hint in Beattie's voice. This was just between the two of them, and Beattie wanted to keep it that way.

'No, I think I'll just manage it by myself,' she said at length.

'That's good, Miss Duff.' The older woman sounded thankful. 'I shan't feel easy about it till I know if the girl is Miss Beryl, and why she's living like that. We don't want to give her away if she prefers to keep herself private.'

'Of course,' agreed Jenny. 'Don't worry, Beattie. I'll be discreet.'

'I know you will, Miss Duff,' Beattie told her warmly. 'If Miss Beryl needs help, I can think of no one better to give her a hand than yourself.'

* * *

But Jenny's visit to Glasgow had to be postponed for a week, when Robin called in to see them on Thursday evening.

'Are you very busy, Jenny?' he asked anxiously, 'or could you help me at all . . . or rather my mother?'

'I'll be glad to help you, if I can,' she said readily. 'What's the matter, Robin?'

He was looking rather white and worried.

'It's this spell of frost, I'm afraid. Mother came home from Ayr by bus this afternoon and slipped as she walked down the road. She's . . . she's twisted her ankle and given herself a shake-up.

I . . . I was wondering if you could come across and see her.'

Beattie had been listening with concern.

'I'd better come, too,' she decided. 'She'll maybe need some help in the house. Is she in bed, Mr. Robin?'

'On the settee, I'm afraid, though she should be in bed. But you know what Mother is like . . . '

Quickly all three hurried back to The Whins, and Jenny could see the reason for the concern on Robin's face as soon as she set eyes on Mrs. Maxwell. Her normally healthy skin had a pale clear pallor and there were dark shadows under her eyes. The nurse had already visited her, and her ankle was well strapped up.

'Dr. Neilson says I should be in bed,' she admitted, 'but I'm better down here. I'd only lie up there feeling sorry for myself.'

'You'll maybe be more sorry for yourself if you don't go to bed,' said Beattie darkly, 'and don't you worry about doing a hand's turn in the house. I can see to it all till you're on your feet again. Miss Duff won't mind, I'm sure.'

'Of course I won't,' said Jenny, and sat down beside Mrs. Maxwell, taking her hand.

'What can I do to help?'

The older woman's eyes filled suddenly with tears.

'You're a good girl,' she said huskily. 'I wish . . .'

She glanced at Robin, who turned away quickly and said he would help Beattie in the kitchen.

'Yes?' asked Jenny.

'Never mind. Only an old woman's fancy. No, dear, I just wanted to ask if you'd take my place on Saturday afternoon at the Church Hall. I've organised a Bring and Buy Sale, with tea and cakes. We're trying to raise money for a new organ, you see.'

Jenny nodded. How busy Mrs. Maxwell was, helping with all these events, yet it took someone like her to organise them, and give others a lead.

'Can you take my place, dear?' she asked.

For a moment Jenny's eyes registered consternation.

'But I wouldn't know what to do!' she protested.

'You don't really have to do anything much,' Mrs. Maxwell told her. 'Just sort out problems as they come up, and collect the money from each stall. Just use your intelligence, my dear. Here, I've written down a full list of all the points you've got to look out for. If you follow that list, you can't go wrong.'

Jenny took it, and her heart quailed a little. It looked rather complicated to her, but she wouldn't let Mrs. Maxwell down.

'Very well, I'll do it,' she agreed.

Her eyes met Beattie's as the older woman came in carrying a tray with Robin bringing up the rear. She gave a small nod, and Jenny knew that the matter of Beryl McLean must be shelved for a little while longer.

'I've made you one or two wee sandwiches,' she told Mrs. Maxwell. 'Mr. Robin says you've been eating like a bird.'

'Robin should stop fussing,' said his mother, though there was a soft look in her eyes. 'I hope you'll all help me to eat them.'

'Just a biscuit,' said Beattie firmly. 'Miss Duff and I have had tea. No, Mrs. Maxwell, you eat up. You mustn't let your strength go.'

Mrs. Maxwell smiled and relaxed. For a little while she was thankful to have Beattie in charge.

Jenny was very much aware of Robin sitting beside her, and she longed to comfort him, but didn't quite know how. Suppose she did find Beryl McLean in Glasgow? How would that affect Robin? she wondered. If the other girl was in trouble, then wouldn't he want to help all he could?

Jenny's thoughts were rather chaotic, but she knew she would be glad to see Robin happy. If she could help in any way, then she would do it. But if finding Beryl McLean was going to hurt Robin . . . if it was Jim Paterson she wanted . . . then what? Jenny's eyes were solemn, but she knew she would have no peace till she solved the mystery, whatever the outcome was likely to be.

* * *

It seemed a long time till the following weekend when Jenny was again on the train for Glasgow. She had gone to help out at the Bring and Buy Sale, and had rather nervously taken Mrs. Maxwell's place, hoping no one would notice her lack of confidence.

But everyone had welcomed her warmly, full of sympathy for Mrs. Maxwell, and Jenny had found that the previous good organising had ensured that the sale ran itself, and there was little for her to do.

She looked around for Carol McLean, and didn't know whether to be glad or sorry when she didn't see her. Jenny didn't know what she could have said to the other girl. Steven had settled down again into his quiet acceptance of everything, but Jenny didn't like the way he was inclined to hang about by himself, and not mix in with the other children. She had grown to love the little boy and she felt he cared for her, too, and now there was a barrier between them, even if it was as fine as glass.

Robin had thanked her warmly for helping his mother, and coming over to keep her company in the evenings. She had got over her first shock, and was now resting quite contentedly with a book.

Beattie was in her element, sorry for Mrs. Maxwell's accident, but delighted to be in a position to help the other woman. She cleaned and polished the house, cooked small nourishing meals, and kept up a run of encouraging conversation.

'It was maybe a blessing in disguise,

Mrs. Maxwell. If you ask me, you were needing a good rest and had to sprain your ankle to get it. Folks that don't rest are sometimes made to rest, that's what I always say.'

'Yes, Beattie.'

'You were looking tired for a while, I thought, and you look more rested now. Here, I'll just put this cushion behind you.'

Mrs. Maxwell accepted these administrations meekly. She knew they were giving Beattie more pleasure than they gave herself.

Robin caught Jenny's eye and grinned rather impishly.

'Thanks for your help,' he told her quietly. 'It's good of you to spare the time.'

'I enjoy coming to talk to your mother,' said Jenny honestly. 'She's a delightful person to know.'

'She's not so bad,' said Robin, not too successfully concealing his pride. 'I wondered, though, if we couldn't go out somewhere next Saturday? The theatre might be a nice change.'

Jenny bit her lip, her face downcast. It would have been lovely to go out with Robin, but she felt she must resolve the other matter of Beryl McLean, especially now that Beattie was also anxious to have it straightened out.

'I'm sorry,' she said hesitantly. 'I'm going to Glasgow for the weekend, I'm afraid. That is, so long as your mother is all right, and doesn't want me . . .'

'Don't worry about Mother,' Robin broke in quickly. 'You have your own life to live, Jenny.'

There was an awkward silence while his eyes rested on her, and Jenny didn't feel capable of offering explanations.

'I hope you have a nice time then,' said Robin.

'Er . . . it's business,' said Jenny, rather lamely.

'Of course.'

But Robin plainly believed that she was bound to be mixing business with pleasure.

Now she tried to put him out of her mind and concentrate on the business in hand. She had telephoned Mrs. Todd, who was only too pleased to fix her up with a room overnight.

'Will you be seeing Mr. Cairns?' Beattie had asked again, rather anxiously.

'No,' decided Jenny. 'As I said before, I'd rather see to this on my own.'

There was no real need to let Charles know since she was only going for one purpose, and it would only complicate matters if she had to keep an appointment with him, too. He was still writing her rather possessive letters, and Jenny knew that she would soon have to make it very plain to him that she could never marry him. She couldn't fall in love with him now, when she was already in love with someone else.

* * *

It was rather cold and wet when Jenny finally arrived in Glasgow, and for a moment she felt she would have welcomed Charles being there to meet her, since she suddenly felt rather lonely. However, she soon pulled herself together, and decided to get a taxi out to the janitor's house.

Mrs. Todd was glad to see her again. She was a quiet, grey-haired woman, who kept her home sparkling clean, and would no doubt have met with Beattie's approval.

'I've got high tea for you, Miss Duff,' she said, with a smile. 'I hope that suits you.'

'It suits me fine, Mrs. Todd,' said Jenny, feeling more relaxed.

'Er . . . you'll not be staying till Sunday, then?'

'I . . . I'm not really sure, Mrs. Todd. I'm here on business, you see, and I don't know how long it will take.'

For all her quietness, Mrs. Todd was blessed with healthy curiosity, but she knew she wasn't likely to be enlightened.

'I've put a hot water bottle in your bed,' she remarked. 'I hope you'll be warm enough.'

'Lovely,' said Jenny, appreciating the blazing kitchen fire. 'It's good of you to have me, Mrs. Todd.'

That night she had difficulty in getting off to sleep, her mind twisting and turning with plans for the following day. Would it be better to call at the restaurant and ask for Miss McLean ... no, it would be Miss Manson ... or to go as a customer, then ask the girl if she could see her later?

Jenny debated the point, then finally fell asleep without really knowing what she was going to do. Suppose this girl really was Beryl? What would she say to her then? She had really got no right to interfere in another girl's affairs, asking her why she was behaving like this.

Then she remembered the little boy. Hadn't she got some sort of responsibility towards the child?

Memory of his quiet little face again

hardened her resolution, so that next morning, she felt she couldn't wait to visit the restaurant at the normal lunch time. She would go about eleven o'clock, and ask to see Miss Manson. If it wasn't convenient for the girl to talk to her, then she would make another appointment.

* * *

Jenny had to wait for about a quarter of an hour before the girl she wanted to see arrived. It was the longest fifteen minutes of her life, but at last she saw the now familiar slender figure walking towards her.

'Miss Manson?'

Jenny stepped forward and the girl looked at her, a hint of alarm in her eyes.

'I . . . I wondered if I might have a private word with you. It's a personal matter.'

'Well, I haven't much time . . . '

'It's very important.'

The girl eyed her, a trifle anxiously, then asked her to wait while she went to have a word with an older woman with carefully set blue-rinsed hair. A moment later she was back.

'In here,' she said, opening a door into a small room. 'How can I help you?'

Jenny's mouth felt dry, but she faced the other girl unwaveringly.

'By telling me if you're really Beryl McLean from Lethansea,' she said quietly.

The colour left the other girl's face.

'Who are you?' she asked shakily.

'Jenny Duff. I'm the temporary teacher at Lethansea.'

The other girl sat down, her hands trembling visibly.

'I . . . I don't want to upset you,' Jenny said quickly. 'Only I have my reasons for trying to find you.'

'Who told you I was here? Neil? It couldn't be Neil . . . he'd have contacted me himself . . . '

'I saw you,' Jenny said quietly. 'I

came here with . . . with a friend of mine and shortly afterwards I saw your photograph. I . . . I thought it was you, but I couldn't be sure.'

'I see.'

Beryl was still looking white and shaken, though a little colour was gradually returning to her cheeks.

'Then no one knows, but you, that I'm here?'

'Not really. Only Beattie . . . Mrs. Sinclair. Her nephew saw you. He's working here in Glasgow.'

'But I mean . . . it isn't common knowledge in Lethansea?'

Jenny shook her head, and saw relief in Beryl's eyes, watching her body gradually relax.

'Why?' she asked. 'Why are you here when everyone thinks you're with your sister in Canada?'

'It's . . . it's a personal matter,' Beryl told her, firmly. 'Miss Duff, it's important to me that everyone thinks I went on holiday. Will . . . will you give me away?'

Jenny bit her lip, looking into Beryl's pleading eyes.

'Don't you want to know why I've come?'

Beryl blinked. 'I thought . . . it was to check up . . . '

'No, it was because of Steven.'

'Steven!' Beryl's face paled. 'What about Steven? He's all right, isn't he? Neil . . . my brother . . . is the only one who knows I'm here. He . . . he said Steven was fine . . . keeping well and going to school . . . '

'But as highly strung as a violin,' said Jenny quietly. 'I'm sure he's worrying about you. Either he thinks you're deliberately neglecting him, or that something has happened to you.'

Beryl said nothing, though her face was very pale again.

'Neil has been giving him small presents from me, and at Christmas . . . '

'At Christmas he expected a present in keeping with his aunt's trip to Canada . . . an Indian outfit, also a Canadian stamp on his Christmas card. It may seem a small thing, but that was important to him. It was his friend Tommy . . . '

'I never thought,' Beryl whispered. 'I . . . I've been so worried, so intent on . . . on staying here quietly. I should have known. I . . . I love Steven, Miss Duff, and it was for his sake, as much as anyone's, that I *didn't* go to Canada. But I should have seen that this would happen. It's . . . it's all my fault . . . '

'Can't you tell me about it?' asked Jenny gently. 'Was . . . if it's anything to do with Robin Maxwell or . . . or Jim Paterson, then . . . then I'm sure they both still . . . '

She broke off. She was now touching on very personal matters which were none of her business. Beryl's face had now gone scarlet, and tears rushed to her eyes.

'I can't talk any longer,' she said, rather thickly. 'Look, Miss Duff, are you going back to Lethansea this afternoon, or could I see you for an hour or two?'

'My time is all yours,' Jenny told her. 'I'll stay as long as is necessary.'

'I can get away for an hour and a half at about three o'clock,' said Beryl hurriedly. 'Can you meet me outside here?'

'I'll be glad to,' Jenny told her, then paused, rather awkwardly. 'Please don't feel obliged to tell me anything, Miss McLean,' she said quietly, 'if you'd rather not. I know it's none of my business, really, and the only thing I want is help for Steven. If you can give me that, then I shall say nothing about meeting you here to anyone. I shall have to tell Beattie, of course, but I know she'll also keep it confidential.'

'Thank you,' Beryl nodded. 'I'll think it over and decide what to do before three o'clock.'

★ ★ ★

Jenny decided to go back to Mrs. Todd's to rest for a couple of hours before meeting Beryl. She had a quick lunch, but she wanted to freshen up and change her shoes. Glasgow pavements were harder to the feet, she decided, than the soft springy turf around Lethansea.

As she walked, rather tiredly, into the small sitting-room of the janitor's cottage, a tall figure rose to greet her.

'Charles!' she cried. 'What are you going here?'

'I think I ought to ask you the same question, Jenny,' he told her coldly. 'I came along to see Daniel Todd, and Mrs. Todd has just told me you're here for the weekend. I must say I was very surprised, Jenny, very surprised indeed. I don't remember your mentioning that you'd be here this weekend.'

'I didn't,' she told him. 'I only decided to come during the week. I . . . I'm here on business, Charles.'

'Business! You mean . . . you might be selling the house? I think this is very inconsiderate of you, Jenny, to do anything about it without consulting me.'

Jenny's eyes began to sparkle. She was tired and worried, and now she felt impatient with Charles.

'It wasn't the house,' she said crossly. 'It was a private matter, and nothing to do with you.'

'Nothing to do with me! Surely you realise by now that your interests are my interests. I have asked you to marry me . . . '

'And I said no, Charles,' said Jenny, very quietly.

'But I asked you when you were upset and needing a change,' he protested. 'I was glad when you went to that little village, to give you time to think over your position. I thought you'd see the future clearly for both of us, here in Glasgow, as my wife . . . '

Jenny drew a deep breath. She hated hurting Charles who had often been good to her and helpful in the past, but now she saw she would have to be very firm, and that she should have been brave enough to make it all clear to him before this. His own wishful thinking was refusing to accept that she really meant it when she turned him down.

'I can't marry you, Charles, ever,' she said clearly. 'I don't love you . . . '

'But we'd grow to love each other. The best marriages are often based on mutual trust and respect.'

'I don't love you, Charles,' she repeated. 'I love someone else.'

'Someone else!' This time Charles' face flushed scarlet. 'So you've been carrying on with someone behind my back!'

This time Jenny leapt to her feet, her eyes sparkling with fury. She had never looked more lovely, and Charles drew back, almost as if he were seeing her for the first time.

'Please go,' she said quietly. 'I thought we could be friends. Now I see that we can't. My life is my own and I shall live it as I please. We have no claim on each other, no claim at all.' She softened for a moment. 'I'm sorry about this, Charles. I thought I'd made myself clear before.'

'Who is it?' he asked jealously.

'It doesn't matter. He doesn't love me, anyway.'

'But I do,' said Charles eagerly. 'Oh, Jenny darling, I didn't realise how much. I do love you.'

She shook her head. 'It's no use, Charles. Please believe me, it's just no use. Please don't ask me again.'

She saw his face change, and he suddenly assumed a dignity she hadn't seen before. For a moment she felt a twinge of regret, feeling that part of her life had now been cut off.

'Goodbye, Jenny,' he said quietly. 'Good luck with your . . . er . . . business.'

'Goodbye, Charles.'

She watched him go, then sat down shakily. It had been one of the most upsetting days of her life. And it wasn't over yet!

* * *

Beryl McLean, wearing a pale grey military-style coat, looked very smart when she met Jenny that afternoon.

'I have a room near here,' she said, 'and my landlady is likely to be out. We can go there and talk.'

The room was in a small flat, though they had to climb three flights of stairs to reach it. Jenny shivered a little in the chilly dampness of the landing, while Beryl produced her key, and thought about Lethansea, wondering yet again what had induced Beryl McLean to come here.

The door opened into a small room, rather garishly bright, but very clean.

'Mrs. McNair works, too,' Beryl told her. 'She won't be home until seven, so we'll be quite private. This is my room.'

Again it was small, but bright with flowered linoleum and scarlet-patterned rugs. Again Jenny felt a twinge, however. Her own lovely room in Howlett Cottage was so much nicer. She knew she would find the large pink roses on the wallpaper rather oppressive after a time. Beryl caught her looking at them, and smiled wryly.

'One gets used to them after a while,' she said simply. 'Mrs. McNair won't mind us using the sitting-room. She's really very good, and I'm lucky to have her. I'll just make a cup of tea, and I've some biscuits here, if that will do.'

'Thank you,' said Jenny. She didn't really want any tea and biscuits, but she felt it would help to relieve any tension.

A short time later Beryl came to sit down opposite to her, and handed her a cup of tea.

'Do you like Lethansea?' she asked.

'I love it.'

For a moment their eyes met and Jenny saw a sudden flash of pain in the other girl's eyes.

'So do I,' she said quietly, then after a moment, 'I hardly know where to begin. It's not really my story, either, but I feel I must tell you.'

She looked at Jenny thoughtfully.

'I don't think you can help . . . except by listening and respecting my confidence, Miss Duff.'

'Please call me Jenny.'

Beryl smiled and Jenny could see why everyone called her beautiful. Already she could feel the charming personality of this girl.

'Jenny,' she repeated softly, 'and my name is Beryl. My parents are dead, but I have a sister, Nancy, who is married and living in Canada. Until I came here, I'd been living in my old home, Westerhouse, with my brother Neil and his wife Carol. You've met them?'

Jenny nodded. 'I went to see them about Steven.'

Beryl nodded, her face whitening.

'And, of course, with Steven,' she continued. 'Nancy and I wrote to each other regularly, and she asked me some time ago to arrange a visit to Canada. It was going to be expensive, but Nancy had more money than I, so she sent me some money to add to my savings, until finally I had enough for my trip to Canada. It was a good sum, but I had only just enough to fly from Prestwick, buy extra clothes, and live comfortably with Nancy for about eight months.

'Then all my friends in Lethansea got up a concert, and gave me a wonderful cheque for my holiday.'

Jenny watched Beryl bite her lip as she remembered.

'I know about the concert,' she said gently. 'It was the photograph taken there which I saw . . . and I recognised you . . .'

Beryl nodded. 'I was so happy. Everyone was wonderful to me. I was all ready to go and only had to pick up my ticket . . .' She got up abruptly. 'Like some more tea?' she asked sharply.

Jenny didn't want it, but after a brief pause she nodded.

'Please.'

Beryl poured for both of them, then continued clearly.

'Before I left I'd had one or two business letters to deal with, but I opened one of Neil's by mistake. It was from his bank. It . . . it was a big shock to me. He . . . he was obviously in financial difficulty, and I began to remember how worried he'd been of late. I knew he hadn't been too enthusiastic about my going to Canada, but I wondered if it was because of Steven.

'Steven was inclined to cling to me, and Carol was jealous. She found it hard to pet the child, and I found it easy, so Steven . . . he used to hang on to me, and Neil didn't like it. I . . . I thought it would be good to go away, and give Steven a chance to settle down with his parents, and he might start clinging to his mother, which he should always have done. I . . . I should have done that years ago, but I was too young to see it at the time. Besides, under my father's will, I can make my home at Westerhouse until I marry.

'However, Neil got impatient when Steven became awkward about my leaving him. It was something we . . . we hadn't resolved, though I tried to reassure Steven that I was only going for a short while, and Mummy and Daddy would be there to look after him. I said I . . . I'd tell him all about Canada . . . all sorts of interesting things . . . '

Jenny drank her tea, saying nothing. Beryl was now talking rather more evenly, and seemed to be finding it easier.

'I taxed Neil with the letter,' she continued, 'and asked him about the business. He admitted he was in difficulties, and was very shocked that the bank would no longer support him, even for a small sum, and angry with me for opening the letter which was marked private. I'd been too excited to notice. He had a contract to fulfil, but he needed ready cash . . . ' Beryl drew a deep breath. 'So I gave him the money for my holiday,' she said simply. 'He needed it more than I.'

Jenny stared, not quite able to understand.

'But . . . but why didn't you just stay

on at home, then?'

'After the concert?' asked Beryl chokily. 'After all those kind people had given me money for my holiday? How could I explain that I had given it to Neil, without telling everyone that the business was rocky. That sort of thing wouldn't have put it on its feet.'

'But . . . but everyone began to worry about you . . . your special friends like Robin and Jim . . . '

'I know.' Large tears were now welling up in the other girl's eyes.

'Nancy refused to help by posting letters. She was furious with Neil, and with me for giving him the money, even if he swore it was only a temporary loan and he could soon give me some of the money back again so that I could still have the holiday, and no one would know. I couldn't write to Robin, or to Jim, without giving it away that I was still in Glasgow.'

'No, I can see that,' said Jenny. 'But why come here . . . I mean, why do this job?'

'I couldn't take a teaching job, or Adam would have been asked for references, and without any other training, I had to take what I could get. I thought this wouldn't be noticeable. No one in Lethansea is likely to come to a small restaurant away from the city centre. I thought no one was likely to see me in this district. But . . . well, it's a small world. I hadn't reckoned on you, or Beattie's nephew.'

She looked at Jenny curiously.

'You must have a wonderful memory for faces. I mean, I'm rather an ordinary-looking person.'

Jenny could have disagreed with her, but she knew it was the incident with Charles, because of Beryl's early incompetence, which had fixed her face in her mind. She didn't wish to explain this to Beryl, so she merely smiled, and nodded.

'I saw the photograph shortly afterwards,' she explained.

There was silence for a while.

'Steven was upset when he didn't get

his Indian outfit at Christmas,' she said after a while, 'and no stamp.'

'I thought the stamp on Nancy's card would have been enough.'

'He was passing them round his friends,' Jenny told her. 'No doubt they scoffed a little when he received none. Children can be cruel to each other.'

'I know.' Beryl's eyes were dark with worry. 'I didn't promise him an Indian outfit, though I think I probably told him tales about Indians when I talked about Canada. It . . . it just didn't occur to me, or I'd have written Nancy about it. I . . . I thought I'd chosen a suitable gift for him, but Christmas was a miserable time for me. I was still getting used to the job, and finding it hard, and I couldn't buy gifts for my friends as usual . . . ' She looked appealingly at Jenny. 'Are they all well?' she asked. 'Robin Maxwell, and . . . and Jim Paterson?'

'Quite well,' said Jenny, trying not to feel a twinge of jealousy. As

Beryl talked, her expressive face had fascinated Jenny, and it was easy to see why both Jim and Robin had wanted her.

Nevertheless, it wasn't fair of Beryl to keep them in the dark.

'I . . . I rather think they were hurt not to hear from you,' she said bluntly, and Beryl flushed crimson.

'I know,' she said huskily. 'It . . . it was the hardest thing I've ever had to do. It was only when . . . when I left that I realised what it was like to be in love . . . '

This time she had to reach for her handkerchief, and Jenny felt her heart go out to the girl. Could she have been brave enough to make the same decision as Beryl? she wondered. Could she have given up such a wonderful holiday, and hidden away here, just to help Neil McLean over a bad patch?

'I had to save the business,' Beryl was saying, rather chokily. 'Neil isn't a fool. He was just going through a bad time, and he'll soon pull straight.

You see, it will be Steven's one day, too. My father worked hard to build it up, and he wanted something which could be a sort of heritage. I . . . I had to do it for Father and Steven, as well as for Neil.'

Jenny nodded, understanding. But should Beryl have sacrificed her love?

'And your own life . . . your own love . . . was that of less importance?' she mused.

'I . . . I thought if he really did love me, he . . . he'd wait,' said Beryl, very quietly, and again Jenny felt a stab of pain.

Was it Robin, or was it Jim? she wondered. She tried to find words to ask, but her tongue seemed unable to form the question. Anyway, she thought rather tiredly, did that really matter? Both men wanted Beryl, and even if it were Jim and not Robin, he was hardly likely to give her the sort of love she would want for marriage, if he couldn't have Beryl.

'Are you still staying on here then?'

she asked. 'It's almost three months yet before you are due back in Lethansea.'

'I don't know,' said Beryl. 'I'd say yes if it weren't for Steven . . .'

The clock began to chime the hour, and she looked up, startled.

'Oh goodness, I must hurry back to work!'

'Of course,' said Jenny, standing up.

'Look,' Beryl said hurriedly, 'are you going back today or tomorrow?'

'I can stay on until tomorrow.'

'Then let me think about it. Can we meet tomorrow afternoon about two? We'll have to go into the nearby park because Mrs. McNair is at home all day on Sunday and likes what she calls a 'good do'. I often walk in the park.'

'Two o'clock tomorrow, then,' said Jenny. 'I'll see you then.'

They left the flat together and parted with a small wave, out in the street.

Jenny turned and watched Beryl McLean till she was out of sight. She could still feel the warmth of the other girl's personality, and kept turning the story Beryl had told her over and over in her mind. If Beryl went back now, she could reassure young Steven that she hadn't deliberately hurt him, and hadn't just vanished out of his life. On the other hand, how could she explain what she had done without hurting her brother, and risking the loss of people's confidence in his business?

Jenny walked back to the janitor's house slowly and thoughtfully. If she were Beryl, what would she do? Jenny had to admit that she didn't know.

* * *

The following afternoon when Jenny met Beryl McLean in the park, she found the other girl pale but rather more composed, as she greeted her with a warm smile.

'Hello, Jenny.'

'Hello, Beryl. Do you want to walk round, or shall we sit down?'

'We can walk round, then sit down

later if it isn't chilly.'

They walked slowly and rather silently, then Beryl slipped a hand through the other girl's arm.

'I want you to know I appreciate your coming to see me the way you did,' she said warmly. 'You could have treated it all very differently. I'm glad you're looking after Steven, and I feel you can help him, even if my decision isn't going to be much help to you.'

'You mean . . . ?'

'I mean I'm sticking it out here until the end of April. After that I come back to Lethansea, and try to ward off too many questions about my holiday in Canada, even if people think me very rude. They'll think it's gone to my head after a while, and leave me alone. I shall probably gain a quick reputation for being far too 'above myself'.'

Beryl gave a small laugh which sounded a trifle bitter.

'You'll never get away with it,' cried Jenny. 'You're bound to give yourself away that you've never even been out of the country.'

The other girl sighed deeply.

'I suppose so,' she agreed. 'You can't hide the truth for ever, can you? But if I'm found out, then I can drop hints that I did it for . . . for love of someone. That, at least, is true. You see, I must keep Neil and the business out of it at all costs, Jenny.'

Jenny didn't see at all. 'To me Steven comes first,' she argued.

'But it's only three more months,' said Beryl, 'then he'll have me back again. Surely he must be getting used to the fact that I'm away until Easter. If he knows I'm coming back then, he'll be all right. I'll try to find an Indian outfit to bring with me when I come home.'

Jenny was still dubious.

'I can't come home now,' Beryl told her. 'Don't you see that, Jenny? If I do, all this will have been for nothing. Neil's getting orders in, and fulfilling them, and soon it will all be on an even keel again. Bad publicity might ruin that. It would soon get about that he had taken his sister's money, given to her by the village for holiday money. Don't you see what that would do to him, and the business?'

Jenny remembered the small community that was Lethansea.

'They'd be right to be angry,' she said, turning to look at Beryl. 'They gave the money to you, not to Neil.'

'I know,' the other girl said tiredly, 'but I could think of no other way. I had to make up my mind quickly. Neil didn't influence me at all. He was quite ready to face up to his difficulties, but I could see ahead very clearly, and I thought the future more important than the present, and a fabulous holiday for me. If I gave up the holiday, I only hurt myself, and possibly Nancy.'

'Steven, too, in a way.'

'But not in another way,' Beryl insisted. 'This way Steven's future is secure.'

Was she right? wondered Jenny. Was

the future more important than the present? She looked again at the beautiful girl with the lovely soft dark hair who was working hard at a job which was strange to her in order to protect the future of her brother and his family.

'Keep our secret until Easter,' Beryl asked, 'will you, Jenny?'

Jenny didn't hesitate any longer.

'Very well, Beryl, if that's what you want. Do you really think you can weather the difficulties when you come back?'

Sudden tears welled in the dark eyes. 'I shall have to, won't I?' Quickly Beryl blinked the tears away. 'Do you mind if I don't come with you to the station?' she asked. 'I . . . I might meet someone . . . '

'Of course,' said Jenny. 'Don't you feel that you run that risk every day?'

'I have no alternative but to take it,' Beryl said simply, then laughed. 'I used to wonder about a blonde wig and spectacles, but I knew I wouldn't

274

be able to live naturally like that. I can only live each day as I am.'

Jenny nodded, and shook hands as they parted, then on impulse she kissed the other girl's cheek.

'I've got your address,' she said huskily. 'If you're badly needed, I'll send for you, Beryl.'

'If I'm badly needed, I'll come home like a shot,' the other girl promised, and swung away, her hair blowing softly about her face. Jenny watched her out of sight, then noticed that she had left her handkerchief on the park bench. She was about to run after her, then decided to post it instead and stuffed it into her own pocket.

Jenny made her way to the station, her thoughts still troubled. She could only see trouble ahead for Beryl McLean.

275

10

Beattie didn't understand at all when Jenny told her that evening.

'The rascal,' she said angrily, 'that Neil McLean, to take the lassie's fare after her saving up. Och, he's no good to anyone, that one. He was never the man his father was. Old Mr. McLean was a very respected man, and everyone knew his business was a good one.'

'Has the quality dropped, then?' asked Jenny.

'No . . . no . . . ' said Beattie, more slowly. 'I've never heard that, though I'm not exactly in a position to judge. Still, whiles you hear things and pick up information, even if you're not connected with it.'

'Beryl was very concerned that we should keep her secret,' Jenny said earnestly. 'Whether they're doing the right thing or the wrong one, I think we should respect that, Beattie.'

The older woman said nothing.

'It's a daft-like idea to kid on you've gone to Canada, then hide away in Glasgow and come back quite joco. Folks are bound to ask her what it was like and want her to give a talk to the Ladies' Guild. They'll soon guess it isn't all above board when she has to refuse. She's an awful daft lassie, in my opinion.'

'She's a brave one,' said Jenny.

Beattie sat down.

'Aye, she has character, has Miss Beryl. Well, I'll say nothing, Miss Duff. I'll promise you that, though there's trouble ahead for her. Anyone can see that.'

Next day Jenny went back to school and told Adam Paterson, when he asked, that she had had a nice weekend in Glasgow, and had found it very interesting.

'It's good to have a break at this time of year,' he agreed. 'No more problems cropping up?'

She flushed. 'Only the usual ones,' she hedged.

Somehow it seemed all wrong that she should know the truth about Beryl, but that Adam Paterson should still be kept in the dark.

'Jean hopes you'll be free to have supper with us again one evening very soon.'

'Thank you,' said Jenny, again rather awkwardly.

'See you later then,' Adam told her cheerfully.

★ ★ ★

Jenny couldn't help paying particular attention to Steven that morning. The little boy looked so neat and clean beside some of the more robust children and Jenny would like to have seen him running freely with the other boys at playtime, instead of always hanging back a little.

'Don't you want to play ball, Steven?' she asked gently. 'I'm sure Tommy and

278

the others would like you to join in.'

He shook his head, his chin going down to rest on his chest.

Jenny sighed. 'It won't be too many weeks until Easter, Steven,' she said softly, 'then your Aunt Beryl will be home again.'

This time the small boy pulled away.

'She won't!' he muttered. 'She won't come back at Easter.'

Jenny paused, staring at the child thoughtfully, then she took his hand, guiding him into the empty classroom.

'Is that what you've been thinking, darling?' she asked. 'Are you worried that your Aunt Beryl will stay in Canada?'

Steven's face began to go red.

'She isn't in Canada,' he told her clearly, and suddenly threw himself into her arms, sobbing convulsively.

Jenny stared, wondering how the child had found out.

'What do you mean, Steven?' she asked, smoothing his hair away from his forehead.

'She's gone away for always,' said Steven chokily. 'Aunt Beryl's gone away for always and isn't coming back.'

'That's nonsense,' said Jenny firmly. 'Whatever made you think such a thing? Of course she's coming back.'

The child sobbed quietly for a moment.

'She said . . . said she'd send me letters and . . . and cards and . . . and things, and I only get letters from Daddy. She's . . . she's not coming back, ever.'

Jenny felt too distressed to think clearly.

'She is coming back,' she insisted. 'I saw her only yesterday and she said she's coming back at Easter.'

The child stared at her, wide-eyed, a tear trembling on his eyelashes.

'Can you keep a secret?' she asked urgently.

Steven nodded, the tear rolling down his cheek.

'Your Aunt Beryl had to go to Glasgow on . . . on business instead of going to Canada. Only she wants to keep it a big secret. She doesn't want to tell anyone.'

The little boy said nothing, gazing at her fixedly.

'So she can't send you letters with stamps on and . . . and other things from Canada, if she isn't there, can she? . . . if she's in Glasgow instead?'

He shook his head solemnly.

Suddenly Jenny remembered that she had Beryl's handkerchief in her coat pocket.

'Wait, Steven,' she said quickly. 'I'll show you something.'

She hurried to her coat, and lifted out the handkerchief, which was pale blue with a large 'B' on the corner.

'See, darling. Aunt Beryl dropped this when we walked in the park. I'm going to send it to her. Shall I send her your love, too?'

A smile began to show through the tears.

'It was for her birthday las' year,' he told her indistinctly.

'You mean . . . you gave her the hankie?'

'I gave her free,' he said proudly.

'Then you know now she's in Glasgow?' she pursued, 'and it's a secret?'

He nodded, and Jenny hugged him again, this time feeling the small arms creep round her neck.

It wasn't until after four o'clock, after a very busy afternoon, that Jenny realised she had had to break Beryl's confidence. But she felt perfectly certain that Beryl would approve wholeheartedly. For the first time in weeks, Jenny saw a new confidence in little Steven and already he was running to the cloakroom with the other boys, as energetic as any of them.

'I had no alternative,' she assured herself. 'I had to tell him.'

It hadn't occurred to any of them that the child was old enough to put such an interpretation on his aunt's silence. But it was easy to see now why the little boy had been so frightened, and had tried to keep those fears to himself. He was much too intelligent not to realise that something was wrong, and his own imagination had done the rest.

Jenny's eyes were dark with worry, however, as she walked home much later than usual, and only acknowledged Robin Maxwell's wave briefly, as he drove past, then stopped.

'It's only a couple of hundred yards, but hop in,' he said, with a smile.

'Not worth stopping,' she commented, but she climbed in obediently.

'How's your mother, Robin?'

'Much better,' he told her brightly, 'not nearly such a bad sprain as we'd feared. Only she insists on hobbling about more than she should. I wish you'd come and give her a lecture. She doesn't listen to me.'

Jenny laughed as the car again slid to a halt. 'I'll try, Robin.'

He reached out and caught her hand as she was about to leave the car.

'Is everything all right now, Jenny?'

he asked quietly. 'You looked rather . . . worried, perhaps, when I saw you walking down the road. Not your usual carefree swing in your step at all.'

'It's all right,' she said hurriedly. 'Don't worry about me, Robin.'

'But I *do* worry about you,' he said, and she was suddenly stilled by the note of urgency in his voice. The soft darkness outside wrapped round the car like a cloud, and she could only see the faint outline of his face.

'I worry about you all the time,' he said, almost with exasperation. 'I know it isn't sensible to fall in love with a girl who's already booked, but that's just what I did, Jenny. I fell in love with you.'

Jenny's breath caught in her throat.

'Oh, Robin,' she whispered, and a moment later she was in his arms, and being held there as though he would never let her go.

'I never thought I'd fall in love like this, Jenny,' Robin told her, against her hair. 'Not after . . .'

'You mean Beryl?' she asked anxiously.

'I don't think we need worry about Beryl,' said Robin. 'I expect she has other plans anyway. I haven't even heard a word from her since she left.'

'But you did care for her?' she asked.

'What's Beryl got to do with us?' asked Robin with annoyance. 'It's you I want, not Beryl McLean.'

'It's just that . . . I thought you were in love with her.'

'I was very fond of her once,' admitted Robin. 'But, Jenny . . . '

She pulled away. 'Let me go a moment, please, Robin,' she said, and he took his arm away immediately.

'Very well,' he said quietly, but her mind felt too confused to see that he was hurt. Would Robin still have fallen in love with her if Beryl hadn't gone away, or if she had been able to keep in touch with him? she wondered. What would happen when she came back at Easter? Would Robin feel differently then?

Jenny felt she couldn't bear it if she accepted his love, only to lose it again. Neither could she keep Robin in her life, if he really belonged to Beryl who had sacrificed enough already . . .

'Is it really Beryl you're worried about, or is it some unfinished business in Glasgow?' he asked rather roughly. 'Is that what you're pushing between us?'

Jenny caught her breath, and thought how close he was to the truth, even if he obviously meant something else.

'I . . . I . . . '

'That's it,' he told her. 'You're a poor liar, Jenny, and I can hear by your voice that I've hit on the truth. You know how I feel, though, and now I'm going to leave you alone. If you want me, you know where to find me.'

He leaned over and opened the car door and she climbed out shakily.

'All right, Robin.'

He drove off without another word. That evening Jenny couldn't sit still, but decided to go for a walk down by the sea, in spite of the cold air and the darkness.

It seemed a long time ago since she had taken this walk, when an early autumn sun had shone over the small village, bathing it in warmth and light. Jenny now wore heavy boots and a thick coat and scarf, but she could still breathe in the tang of the seaweed, and remembered, with nostalgia, the factory where Robin worked. She had been happy the day he showed her round. Then the tangle had reminded her of a lovely old song, which had stuck in her mind for a long time.

Now her life seemed to be caught in a different sort of tangle, one which bound her to the McLeans, then reached out to Robin Maxwell. Beattie, too, was caught in it, and perhaps even the Patersons. How would Jim Paterson feel when Beryl came home? He would want some explanations from her, too. And Robin? If only she could have asked Beryl about who held her heart?

'It was only when I left that I realised what it was like to be in love.'

Jenny remembered Beryl's words, hearing them spoken again as clearly as a bell. Suppose it was Robin . . .

She stumbled on some rough ground and jarred her ankle, the pain searing through her body, to her heart, then she walked home and went straight upstairs to bed.

* * *

Jenny received a polite little note from Neil McLean three days later, asking if she could possibly find time to call at Westerhouse that evening. Any time would do.

She frowned a little, looking at the note and wondering what Mr. McLean could have to say to her. Steven had been a different boy, full of noise and high spirits. She had even had to send him down to the clinic to have his knee bandaged after falling in the playground. His loud roars had been more welcome than the stoic qualities he had previously shown.

But perhaps that was what was wrong. Perhaps Neil McLean, or more probably Carol, was worried about bandaged knees and soiled jerseys. Jenny's chin firmed, and she decided she would be delighted to go to Westerhouse that evening.

The young au pair girl again showed her through to the study where Neil McLean was working steadily, at his desk. He looked up and acknowledged Jenny with a brief nod.

'Good of you to come, Miss Duff. Please sit down and we can talk in just a moment.'

Hastily he checked a few figures, made rapid notes on a few sheaves of paper, then put them away neatly in a folder, before turning again to face Jenny. There was no friendliness in his eyes when he looked at her.

'I'll come straight to the point, Miss Duff. Is it true that you have been seeing my sister in Glasgow?'

Jenny caught her breath, off guard, at the sudden question. She turned scarlet, then caught hold of herself. After all, she had done nothing which could shame her.

'Yes, it is true, Mr. McLean.'

'And you told Steven?'

'I had to. Perhaps you didn't know it, but your son had rather worrying ideas over what had happened to his aunt.'

This time Neil McLean's face changed.

'If my son was worried, surely he would have asked me.'

'Not necessarily, Mr. McLean. A child can worry about things without having any clear idea how to allay his fears. I only found this out by asking him.'

'You seem to have done a lot of asking.'

Jenny rose to her feet.

'I had the child's interests to think of. I think you'll agree that he's much happier now that he knows the truth.'

Neil McLean looked suddenly very tired.

'Please sit down, Miss Duff,' he said quietly. 'Obviously we must discuss this further. You have spoken to my sister? May I ask how you knew she was in Glasgow?'

'I had seen here there before I came to Lethansea, and I recognised her photograph. When . . . when I realised Steven was worrying himself over his aunt, I decided to go and see her.'

'Why didn't you tell me you'd met Beryl before?'

'I wasn't sure she was the same girl . . . then.'

'I see.' Neil McLean leaned forward in his chair. 'Did she tell you why she went to Glasgow?'

Jenny nodded, feeling sudden pity for the man opposite as she began to notice the grey in his hair, and the tired lines on his face.

'You'd be forgiven for thinking me the worst rogue under the sun,' he said, after a long pause.

'It is entirely your affair, and Beryl's,' said Jenny. 'I've promised to say nothing to anyone. Unfortunately I broke that promise over Steven, but I felt it was necessary.'

'Then perhaps you'll understand that sometimes we have to do things abhorrent to us because they are necessary,' said Neil, 'such as I had to do when I did all in my power to save the business. You must appreciate, it wasn't just for my own sake.'

'Beryl said it was for Steven's, too . . .'

'And not just for Steven's, Miss Duff. We are a fairly small firm, but I have very loyal workers, who would have been without a job if McLeans went out of business. They might find it difficult to get other work, and most are men with families. I carry a responsibility for quite a number of people.'

'I see,' said Jenny, beginning to look at Neil McLean in a new light.

'I know I was thinking about myself,

and my own family, too, and that included Beryl who makes her home with us. My father built up the business, and people could say that I've made a poorer job of carrying it on, but those are the people who have no understanding of rising prices and higher costs. When Beryl offered to help, I knew that she'd only be tiding me over a temporary setback, and that I could soon pull straight. I . . . I thought she could still go to Canada to see Nancy, but perhaps for a much shorter time. I'd be able to pay back some of the money at least, with contracts which were coming in.'

'I see.'

Jenny couldn't help feeling sympathy for Neil.

'It was essential that no one should know, because lack of confidence can spread very quickly. So I told no one. Not even Carol, my wife. Nor Steven. Beryl wrote him little notes, and I gave them to him, supposed to be from my letters. I get the post every morning, so Carol didn't suspect. I didn't realise, though, that he wanted the stamps for his friends at school. What small things there are to catch us out! He always appeared to accept his little notes happily, and because he gave no trouble, I thought there was none.'

He was silent for a while, tapping his pen idly on a piece of paper.

'I knew how people would react, what they'd say if it ever got out . . . that I had allowed Beryl to bolster up the business . . . I knew it would finish me. I had to make the decision, and I made it. Now . . . ? Well, maybe it was the wrong thing to do.'

Jenny said nothing. She wasn't at all sure whether the deceit in this case wasn't justified. Neil was leaning towards her.

'Miss Duff, Beryl can still go to Canada . . . '

'What do you mean, still go to Canada?'

Jenny whirled round, seeing the

294

colour leave Neil McLean's face when he saw Carol standing in the doorway. She came into the room and closed the door.

'What do you mean?' she repeated. 'Surely Beryl *is* in Canada? Haven't you been hearing from her, Neil?'

He seemed to be tongue-tied as he looked from Carol to Jenny.

'And what's it go to do with Miss Duff?'

'Sit down, darling,' said Neil, rather hoarsely. 'I can see I'll have to tell you all about it.'

'I'll go,' said Jenny, standing up.

'No,' Carol told her sharply. 'This obviously concerns you, and something's been kept from me. I've been thinking for some time that there was something peculiar going on. Better tell me, Neil.'

Jenny sat on the edge of her chair as Neil began to tell Carol, as briefly as possible, all about Beryl's help for the business, and how she had decided to go to Glasgow.

'I thought I could send her the money, as soon as the contract was completed, and as soon as I was sure of the others coming in. The business was only going through a bad patch, and it's now picking up wonderfully again, Carol darling, so there's no need to worry. I was just telling Miss Duff here that Beryl can still go, even if it's for a much shorter time.'

'I see.'

Jenny looked at Carol McLean to see how she would take this news, which must have come as a shock to her. She had always seemed a rather cold, selfish young woman, and she had listened to the whole story with a cool, impassive expression on her lovely face.

'And that was what was wrong with Steven?' she asked, with an effort, turning to Jenny. 'You say Steven realised something was wrong, and was worrying over it?'

Jenny nodded.

'Then why didn't he tell me . . . his mother? Why did he tell you instead?'

'Children often tell their teachers things, and probably tell their mothers different things they wouldn't mention at school,' said Jenny gently.

'I . . . I thought when Beryl went . . . I . . . I could be a better mother to him. I . . . I find it hard to manage children. It was easier for Beryl. I guess I was jealous . . . then it seemed as though it was even worse than before, though I tried to pretend I was imagining things . . .'

Carol's composure suddenly cracked and she ran over to Neil.

'You should have told me,' she said thickly. 'I could have helped. I know I've been selfish, but I'd have been different, honestly, Neil. I . . . I wouldn't have spent so much . . .'

Jenny rose again to her feet. This time no one stopped her as she slipped out quietly and closed the door. Somewhere she could hear Steven shouting in the garden, and the young au pair girl calling that it was time for bed.

Her step lightened a little as she

walked up the gravel drive. Something told her the McLeans would now be a closer and happier family.

★ ★ ★

Jenny knew she ought to feel happier now that Steven was doing so well at school and her worries had been lessened, but she was still very unsettled in her own life.

She had seen Robin several times, but he had greeted her very politely and rather impersonally. She felt very tempted to tell him all about Beryl, but felt she couldn't tell anyone else without the girl's permission. Already Beattie, her nephew, and the McLean family were all in the secret, which could very easily become a secret no longer. Jenny felt that her part in it was now closed.

She had gone to one or two local events with Jean Paterson, and had been pleased to see Jim again. He had talked to her cheerfully, but she noticed that he often had silent moods, and wondered if he was thinking about Beryl. Most people seemed to have accepted the fact that they hadn't heard from her, and no longer commented on the fact.

On Friday Jenny got a letter with a Glasgow postmark, and opened it eagerly. It was from Beryl.

'Would it be too much to ask if you could come and see me again?' she wrote. 'Neil wrote to me, telling me you'd been to see him, and we're all most grateful that you've respected our confidence.

'But now I'm making fresh plans, because I can still go and visit Nancy, even if it's only for a short time. With Neil's help, and what I've saved from my job in Glasgow, it will be quite possible. I hope to fly from Prestwick on Monday next, and I'd like to see you before I go. Could you possibly come to Glasgow on Sunday? I can meet you in the park again and we can have tea together in the afternoon.'

Jenny decided to show Beattie the note, and explain to her about going back to Glasgow that weekend. She had already told Beattie about her interview with Neil McLean, which had softened the older woman's attitude.

'He had other folk to think of right enough,' Beattie admitted. 'I shouldn't be the one to blame him, because who's to say what I'd have done in his shoes?'

'I know,' agreed Jenny. 'It wasn't an easy decision to make.'

'And maybe it wasn't easy for Neil McLean taking over from his father. They were two different kind of men. He might have been far better doing something else. Och well, Miss Duff, it's none of our business and we'll keep mum about it.'

Now Beattie was obviously delighted that things were turning out all right for Miss Beryl.

'Half a loaf is better than no bread,' she intoned, 'as I always say. She won't have the grand holiday we all thought, but she'll see plenty nevertheless. Tell her she's to be sure and send us all a postcard.'

'I will,' smiled Jenny.

Beryl looked much happier when Jenny met her in Glasgow, and once again they sauntered round the park.

'It's been lovely finding you, Jenny,' Beryl told her, taking her arm. 'I felt so lonely and isolated before you came seeking me out. But now it's good not to have to pretend. I can be myself when I talk to you.'

'I'm glad,' said Jenny simply.

'I've cabled Nancy. She was furious before, but she'll soon come round when I turn up after all, and I'll be able to explain it all to her much more clearly.' She turned rather shyly to Jenny. 'There's just one thing . . . one more person I want you to see for me. I know he'll keep my secret, too. For a time I thought I'd say nothing to him, but that was when only Neil and I knew, and I felt I couldn't tell anyone else. I didn't know what would happen if I wrote to tell him the truth, but now I'm sure it will be all right, especially if you're at hand to answer any questions. I've stressed that he mustn't go bombarding Neil. I don't want him to do that.'

Jenny nodded, feeling rather hollow inside. She watched Beryl producing her letter and her heart beat painfully as she wondered if it was for Robin.

'Would you pass it on for me, Jenny?' asked Beryl. 'It's to . . . Jim Paterson.'

Jenny took the letter, hardly trusting herself to speak.

'Jim proposed to me before I left, but I wasn't sure then. So many exciting things were happening that I felt my emotions weren't in a normal state, though I had always liked him a lot. I felt I was in love with him, but I had to be very sure.' Beryl sat down on a bench and made room for Jenny. 'It was only after I got to Glasgow, when I had time to think, that I realised how much I did care for him. I badly wanted to write and tell him so, but I kept thinking that if we really did care for each other, then he'd wait for me to come home again. Now . . . now I don't want to take that chance. You don't think me foolish, Jenny?'

The other girl shook her head, wondering how to ask the question uppermost in her mind.

'You . . . you weren't special friends with Robin . . . Robin Maxwell?' she asked carefully.

Beryl stared, then her eyes cleared as she understood.

'Robin and I were always good friends and very fond of one another, but only friends, Jenny. At one time we went about together, and I think we both wondered if it wouldn't develop into something deeper. Only it never did. I like Robin a great deal, and I think he likes me, too. But we could never be more to each other.'

'Thank you for telling me,' said Jenny quietly.

'Good luck,' Beryl told her. 'When

I come back from my holiday, I hope we'll see a lot of each other.'

'I hope so, too,' smiled Jenny.

★ ★ ★

Jenny travelled back in the train, her emotions very mixed. The precious letter to Jim Paterson was in her handbag, but her whole mind was centred on Robin.

She had made an awful mistake, she thought unhappily. Robin had told her he loved her, but she hadn't trusted him enough to believe it. She had thought it was because he was trying to put Beryl out of his life, and she would lose that love as soon as he saw Beryl again. Now she bit her lip, her eyes solemn as she began to realise how wrong she had been, and her heart went cold when she remembered how offhand he had seemed of late.

It was her own fault if she had lost Robin, she thought wretchedly. He'd offered her wonderful happiness, and she hadn't accepted it.

'If you want me, you know where to find me,' he'd told her.

Would it be any use going to see him, she wondered, and telling him how wrong she'd been? She had always believed that mistakes should be put right, and now she had to resolve her own.

That evening, after she had had a hot meal and a rest by the fire, while Beattie fussed over her as she quietly answered a lot of excited questions, Jenny decided to walk over the road to The Whins.

But only Mrs. Maxwell was at home, though she greeted Jenny very happily.

'I'm so glad to see you, Jenny dear. Come in and talk to me for a little while. Robin's out, I'm afraid. He's a restless man these days. I just don't know what's got into him.'

'Oh,' said Jenny.

She sat down, nervously, but although Mrs. Maxwell did her best to entertain her visitor, it was obvious that Jenny was ill at ease. She still had the letter to deliver to Jim, and wondered if he was at the school-house this evening. She had promised to deliver it by hand, and give Jim a full explanation, but her first instinct had been to see Robin again. Now she didn't know whether to be glad or sorry that he was out.

'I . . . I'll have to go, I'm afraid,' she apologised, standing up. 'I've got to see the Patersons about . . . something.'

'I understand, dear,' said Mrs. Maxwell, though her eyes were rather puzzled. Jenny wasn't her usual self at all.

★ ★ ★

She was luckier, however, when she reached the schoolhouse and Jean welcomed her into the family circle.

'Oh, I'm glad you're here, Jim,' she smiled. 'I wanted a word with you.'

Then she blushed furiously when she caught the knowing look Adam Paterson flashed at his wife, and Jim's momentary look of embarrassment.

306

'It isn't personal,' she said hurriedly. 'Only . . .'

'If it's private, you can talk in here,' Jean assured her, 'while Adam and I can make a pot of tea. Come on, dear.'

'Oh dear,' said Jenny, her face still hot as she turned to Jim after they had gone. 'I hope they didn't get the wrong impression.'

'Don't bother yourself,' said Jim, obviously relieved. 'You know what Jean and Adam are like for matchmaking. They've probably been throwing me at you for weeks!'

Jenny laughed and reached into her handbag for the letter.

'It would be a waste of time,' she told him. 'Here's something, though, which might interest you.'

Jim's face paled when he saw the writing on the envelope.

'Where did you get it?' he asked hoarsely. 'It . . . it's from . . . Beryl.'

'Yes,' she agreed, smiling. 'It's from Beryl. If you listen for a moment, I'll try to tell you all about it.'

Jim's eyes seemed to burn into hers while she told him the whole story, though she caught a flash of anger when she told him about Neil McLean.

'That's sheer blackmail,' he said roughly. 'For whatever reason, he had no business to let Beryl take responsibility for his shortcomings. I've a good mind to . . . '

'I know,' interrupted Jenny. 'That's why Beryl kept it from you, and gave me the job of telling you instead of just writing. She doesn't want you to go rushing off to Neil. She asked me to make that clear. Please believe me, Jim, it would only upset her. And I think she deserves a carefree holiday now, don't you?'

'When does she leave?' Jim asked, his eyes suddenly blazing.

'Tomorrow afternoon . . . from Prestwick.'

'Then I'll try to see her off,' he told her, and she could sense his excitement at this unexpected sight of Beryl, even if it was only for a short time.

'I'll leave you to read your letter,' said Jenny, seeing him slip it into his jacket pocket.

'Here's Jean with the tea. I . . . I'll read it later, Jenny.'

She nodded, her eyes soft. She understood perfectly.

★ ★ ★

Jenny did her best to settle into routine the following day. It was now February, her least favourite month, redeemed in her opinion only because it was short. It always seemed to her a time of waiting, and should have been a time of rest.

But she didn't feel at all like resting. Soon, very soon, she would leave Lethansea for good. Beattie kept insisting that she must keep coming back at holiday times, and she had already promised Beryl that she would keep in touch. But she knew that she would only want to come back if Robin wanted her. If he didn't want her any more, then she'd be better to make a clean break, and try to take up the threads of her life, again, in Glasgow.

In the evening she asked Beattie for the use of the kitchen table, as she began to prepare a project for her children.

'They are all going to write a poem about spring,' she told Beattie, 'and the best poems will be pinned up on this long piece of card. I'll prepare it, then the children can make lambs and spring flowers to stick on. They enjoy things like this.'

'So they should,' said Beattie approvingly. 'There was none o' that in my day. All we got was the three R's and the strap if we got it wrong. Mind you, it made us learn, and no nonsense.'

Her tone indicated that she wondered if Jenny's children learned as much, but Jenny didn't feel like getting involved in one of Beattie's debates.

'I'll leave you to it, then, Miss Duff,'

the older woman told her. 'I'm going down to help with a jumble sale. Mrs. Maxwell needs me, because she's still not a hundred per cent, and I can give her a good hand provided she tells me what to do.'

'That's good,' said Jenny, half guiltily.

She should maybe have offered her services, too, though Beattie assured her it wasn't at all necessary.

'You've your own work to do,' she said flatly. 'We older ones have to make jobs for ourselves at times.'

Jenny was busy working on her project when the bell shrilled, and she wiped her paint-stained fingers on a piece of cloth before going to open the door.

'Hello, Jenny,' said Robin.

The quick colour rushed to her cheeks as she stepped back to invite him in.

'I . . . I'm just preparing a long piece of thick card for a project,' she explained confusedly. 'I . . . I'm working in the kitchen, Robin.'

He came through to the small cosy kitchen, and dropped rather tiredly into a comfortable armchair.

'Don't let me interrupt, Jenny. Carry on with your work . . . please do. What's it going to be anyway?'

She explained slowly at first, then more easily, and her small face grew animated as she told him how the children would be encouraged to help.

'You like teaching, don't you, Jenny?' he asked quietly.

'Love it,' she said simply.

'Your life's work?'

Robin's question had been light, but now he turned to her seriously.

'Your life's work, Jenny? Is that it? Are you hoping to carry on teaching in Glasgow even . . . if . . . if you decide to marry one day?'

She didn't look away, though again she could feel her heart beating painfully.

'I could give it up,' she said huskily, 'for the right reason.'

'For what reason?'

'Marriage . . . to the right person. I'm not in love with Charles Cairns, Robin, and I shan't ever marry him.'

'And Jim Paterson?' he asked, catching her arm.

'I . . . I think he's going to marry Beryl McLean,' she said breathlessly. 'I never fell in love with Jim, but I thought you'd be hurt . . . because of Beryl.'

Jenny's voice became muffled as Robin's arms went round her.

'Why couldn't you have accepted me then, when I asked you before?' he asked, half angrily, then his voice became tender. 'We've wasted time, Jenny darling, and I hate wasting time. I ought to spank you instead of kissing you for being difficult.'

'I'm sorry, Robin,' she told him, her eyes shining with happiness. 'I . . . I couldn't really believe it was me. I mean . . . I'm not . . . '

She broke off. Robin obviously thought her pretty enough, and that was all that mattered.

'You're not going to be awkward again,' he finished, 'though I've noticed at work that sometimes awkward jobs can be the most fascinating.'

Jenny grinned, wondering if she'd always have a little bit of a rival for Robin's affections in his work. Luckily, however, she would probably always be interested enough to share it with him.

'Let's walk down by the sea-front,' she said, taking his hand. 'Let's smell the seaweed, even if it's a different sort from the tangle o' the isles.'

The sea would be doubly precious to her now that it would always be hers, she thought happily.

'Oh, Robin,' she said, as they opened the door to the cold fresh air, 'isn't it lovely to be at home?'